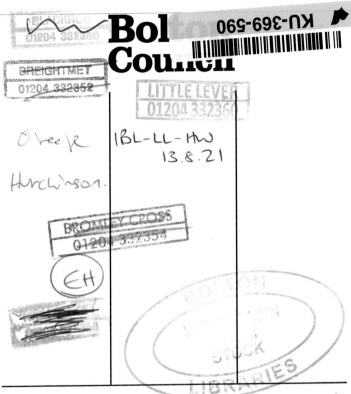

Please return / renew this item
by the last date shown.
Books may also be renewed by
phone or the Internet.

BL

**Tel: 01204 332384**

**www.bolton.gov.uk/libraries**

# The Crooked M Killings

Marshal Reuben Kane is charged with finding the men who have spread terror and violence in an unprecedented bank robbing spree. It's a routine, albeit dangerous, assignment. Routine, that is, until Reuben discovers Sal McIntyre, badly beaten and left to die by the men he is hunting. Near to her is the body of her murdered husband.

Reuben postpones his search in order to nurse the woman back to health, but from the moment she regains consciousness, vengeance is the only thing on her mind. Sal's hatred is all-consuming and, against his better judgement, Reuben finds himself drawn into her ill-conceived plot to kill the men who murdered her husband.

Reuben sets out to bring them to justice. But Sal McIntyre wants revenge. At any cost.

# The Crooked M Killings

Frank Ellis Evans

**A Black Horse Western**

ROBERT HALE

© Frank Ellis Evans 2018
First published in Great Britain 2018


ISBN 978-0-7198-2725-9


The Crowood Press
The Stable Block
Crowood Lane
Ramsbury
Marlborough
Wiltshire SN8 2HR


www.bhwesterns.com


Robert Hale is an imprint
of The Crowood Press

Typeset by
Derek Doyle & Associates, Shaw Heath
Printed and bound in Great Britain by
CPI Group (UK) Ltd, Croydon, CR0 4YY

*To Margaret and RST*

# CHAPTER ONE

# ONE MORNING

It was hot. The sky was cloudless blue and the sun cast short shadows across the landscape and the ranch house. Cattle lay in whatever shade they could find and an elderly horse lapped lukewarm water from a trough. The only sign of purposeful activity was that of a slim, sun darkened man mending a fence. Silence fell when he stopped hammering the nail and wiped his brow. He straightened his back, stretched and looked first towards the sun then to the horizon. In the far distance he noticed a small cloud of dust. Cattle or, more likely, riders from a neighbouring ranch looking for strays before nightfall, he decided.

It had been a relentlessly hot day and his sweat-soaked shirt clung uncomfortably to his body.

'Ed!' a woman's voice called from the veranda. 'Riders coming. About a mile away.' She was a tall, slim, handsome woman in her mid thirties with jet black hair tied back. Her predominant features were large grey eyes in an open, honest face.

'Seen 'em, Sal. Probably Lazy Gopher boys looking for strays. Roy was asking if we'd seen any on our land the other day in town and I told him to send some of his men round. Strange that they're riding in a bunch though. It'd make more sense to spread out and cover more ground.

'Are you off to town to get them supplies yet?'

'Yup.' He grunted acknowledgement, not relishing the idea of a hot two mile ride into Blanca Creek. Reluctantly, he hitched his horse to the rig, occasionally eying the approaching riders.

'I'll have a swill down 'fore I go,' he said and sat on the veranda, idly watching the approaching dust cloud. He reckoned there were at least four riders, maybe more. It was difficult to see through the dust they were creating. They appeared to be travelling fast and he estimated that they would arrive at the ranch in five minutes and he wanted to stay and exchange news with them – visitors were rare and welcome in this isolated place – but he knew he had to go. The woman appeared with a jug of water, poured two drinks and sat down beside him. Sal McIntyre was not the usual rancher's wife. She had met Ed fifteen years ago when he was still helping to build up the ranch which his father had started. At the time she was a sharp-shooter and trick rider in a travelling show which Ed and his father had attended. Ed had been smitten from the moment he saw her. Knowing that they would probably never see each other again after the show moved on, he had seized the opportunity and proposed to her. His father was opposed to the idea, but realizing that his son was determined, John McIntyre had, with marked reluctance, given his consent. 'You're just like your ma was. Cussed and headstrong.' That was all the old man had said and they had married in the white wooden church at Blanca Creek. Initially, the atmosphere in the ranch house had been icy but John wasn't a man to harbour a grudge and he soon realized how hard working and honest his new daughter-in-law was. These qualities, plus her ready smile and her sense of humour quickly won him over. Two years to the day after the wedding, John had been badly hurt in a riding accident and Sal had nursed him for three months until his death, making herself available day and night. Ed and Sal inherited the ranch and through their industriousness and astute planning they built up a fine herd and became reasonably prosperous, even though they did nearly all the work themselves, relying on travelling cowboys only when they were overwhelmed. Sal still practised her shooting skills and she could break a clay pipe in half with one shot from a Colt from twenty feet or hit a moving target with a Winchester with almost super-human accuracy. She was also a very fast draw. On their bedroom wall hung a framed old poster which described her as *Sharp Shooting Sally Seddon. The Fastest Draw Since Billy the Kid!* As the Kid had died at the hands of Pat Garrett some years before, no one had ever questioned the claim and Sal often took on challengers for $10 wagers and had only been outdrawn once, when a gunslinger answering to the name of Abraham Coulson had beaten her by two to one in a best of three. Even now, when she thought about it, it still rankled.The gunplay was, of course, all for show. She had never drawn a gun in anger and had no intention of ever doing so. When she shot animals for the pot on her ranch she always felt sorry for the little critters. Indeed, she even hated shooting vermin on the ranch and whenever possible she left that job to Ed. Ed drained his drink and climbed on to the buckboard. 'See you tonight.' He blew a kiss. 'I'd've liked to share a word or two with the Gopher boys but I can't wait or the store'll be closed afore I get there.' Sal stood and watched as he rode to the arched wooden gate which bore the sign *Crooked M Ranch*. He turned, as always, and waved and she waved back. The riders had almost reached the gate themselves now and from what she could see through the dust there were not four, but seven or eight of them. She'd not seen any of the Lazy Gopher boys, even though it was the nearest ranch to theirs, since its owner Roy Gregory had thrown a party to celebrate his fiftieth birthday. As she squinted into the sun she couldn't recognize any of the horsemen, who had stopped to talk with her husband. The man doing the talking was a gigantic man on a pure white horse. He was powerfully built but flabby. She heard his voice carrying on the air. 'We'd be obliged if you'd let us water our horses, mister.'

'Sure. There's a stream at the back of the ranch. You're welcome to water your steeds and to fill your bottles. Help yourself.' Ed smiled courteously.

'. . . and mebbe some food for me 'n' my boys.'

'Sorry. Can't do. I'm just off to town for supplies. We're low on just about everything. Sal can probably rustle you up a coffee but we've only got a couple of slices of bread and a bit of dried beef.'

The fat man leaned forward and interrupted him. 'I said we're hungry, mister.' He looked around as if trying to spot something and at length he spoke again. 'I can see a good few steers round about. I'm sure that you wouldn't miss one and it would be a real kindly gesture. So how about if'n we said we was *real* hungry.' Ed looked at the

10

men uneasily then met the gaze of the fat man. The threat contained in his words was obvious but Ed continued to smile and spoke in a friendly tone.'I don't know if you know this territory, mister, but you're welcome to ride with me to Blanca Creek. They have a real good place which serves steaks and—'

'My name's Shep Cassidy.' His smile had disappeared and been replaced with a faintly menacing scowl. 'It's a name you'd do well to remember, cowboy. Now I ain't going to ask you again.' So saying, Cassidy slid his rifle out of its holster and took deliberately theatrical aim at the nearest cow. Ed stood up on the cart and launched himself at the rifle, causing it to fire harmlessly into the sky. He never saw the weasel faced man in the floppy sombrero draw his pistol.The shot from the sombrero man's gun hit Ed in the temple and simultaneously Shep Cassidy swung his rifle and fired a single shot. The bullet from the big man's rifle thudded into Ed's chest and he was dead before he even hit the ground. The sombrero man holstered his gun without a sound. Cassidy, showing no emotion, replaced his rifle. Sal started to run back to the house where the guns were kept. With a surprising turn of speed and agility for such a large man, Cassidy whipped his horse into action. She was overtaken by the fat man and he kicked out at her, catching her on the shoulder and causing her to fall. As she scrambled to her feet she saw that his gun was pointing at her head. He was smiling a dour, humourless smile.

'Well, pretty lady. I don't think it'd be wise to try anything hasty.' He gave a cursory nod in the direction of Ed's body. 'I don't think *he's* going to be of assistance. Now stand up and let me see you.' Sal slowly stood up, wincing

11

from the pain in her shoulder where the boot had landed. She showed no fear and stared venomously. Two men dismounted and stood behind Shep. She recognized them from Wanted posters in town as Rab and Johnny Davies. The Davies Brothers, both wanted for robbery and murder, walked towards her and drew their guns.

'You know what I think, pretty lady?' Shep said, with a wide smile. 'I think the boys and me have not seen a woman like you for a good time. I can see that you're hospitable like. Now wouldn't you like to have a bit of fun with me an' the boys?'

He leaned down from the saddle, held her firmly by the hair and ran the fingers of his free hand through her hair tracing a line down to her cheek. She tore herself from his grasp and ran for the house and this time he was too slow, hindered by his enormous girth. She grabbed the Winchester which stood leaning on the door post and turned. Two horsemen had drawn their guns and she fired twice with deadly accuracy. They both fell to the ground. She pulled the trigger for the third time, this time aiming at the fat man, but there was only a click.The gun was empty. With a furious bellow the fat man was upon her. She hissed an oath and spat full in his face. He simply laughed and shoved her, causing her to stumble and almost fall. The other men began to cheer and laugh as the fat man pushed her against the gate. She saw Ed's hammer lying on the floor and grabbed it then swung it in the direction of the big man's face. Too late. The man's heavy punch made contact with her jaw and was followed by another. Everything went black. Cassidy stood over her, breathing heavily due to the exertion. None of his men had moved, even when Sal had shot their two friends.

Cassidy shoved Sal's prone form with his boot and seeing that she was unconscious, he turned to his men.

'That was a fine bit of shooting,' he drawled. 'Did you see that, Pete?'

'Sure did, Shep. Never seen a woman shoot like that afore. Two shots. Two dead. They never knew what hit 'em.' He looked thoughtful but totally unmoved. He scratched his chin then he said, 'Mayhap we should try a bit of target practice. Mebbe if we give her a five-minute start we could see who could hit her first with a Winchester. Waddya think, boss?' Shep appeared not to hear him and knelt down next to Sal's still body before running his hand lasciviously over her thigh. Neither he nor any of the men were moved in any way by the death of their two friends. In fact, apart from confirming that the two were dead and greedily removing guns and valuables from the corpses, the remaining men paid attention only to the woman lying in the dust.

'A fine lookin' woman.' The speaker was the man sitting on his horse furthest away from Sal. He was yellow skinned and saucer eyed. He rarely blinked and had a disconcerting way of staring at people – a habit which had got him into many bar room brawls. He had, over the years, gunned down six men and a boy of twelve. He had killed his first man in an argument over a girl in Tombstone when he was only thirteen years old and after the murder, he had stolen a horse and hightailed out of town in the knowledge that he was a wanted man, or more accurately, a wanted boy. Within days he had gunned down the twelve-year-old, an innocent boy who had caught him stealing from his father's shop. The murdered youngster had been unarmed and posters had soon appeared, offering the outraged populace a reward for capture of the killer. As his name wasn't known, the posters could only base their information on the fact that he was in his early teens and he had staring, black eyes. He had adopted a selection of aliases for some time and had been described on posters as The Black-eyed Boy, but eventually he had been identified as Jed Gambles by a barman in Tombstone. He stared at Sal. 'Fine looking woman,' he repeated softly to himself. 'Don't you think she's a fine looking woman, Shorty?'

The final member of the group was a squat man, no taller than five feet, who spat out some chewing tobacco and tipped his hat back off his forehead. Shorty Gambles was Jed's twin brother, but there was little similarity in looks. Shorty had an almost square face and immensely strong shoulders and a barrel chest and whereas Jed sported a long, drooping moustache, of which he was inordinately proud, Shorty merely had rough stubble. In some respects Shorty was the most vicious of all the men. He enjoyed gratuitous violence and had once smashed a beer glass in the face of a saloon girl then shot her in the stomach simply because she preferred his brother to him. The men climbed down from their horses and gathered round the woman. Pete Robinson, the man in the sombrero and second in command to Shep Cassidy grinned and prodded Sal with the toe of his boot. Pete was known as 'Crazy' Pete Robinson because of his unpredictable and violent nature. It was a nickname which he hated. Even Shep was wary of him, but for the moment Pete was smiling, almost amiably.

'Go to it, big man.' He laughed. 'Go to it.' Sal was dimly aware of the laughing and whooping of the three men as Shep pressed upon her. They seemed to be far, far away.

She smelled sour whiskey and somewhere in her mind she felt a sharp pain before unconsciousness mercifully enfolded her again. Before leaving, the men stripped the house of the remaining food and drink.

# CHAPTER TWO

## REUBEN

Reuben Kane sat on a rickety wooden rocking chair outside the Diamond King saloon. He was a tall, lean man heading towards middle age and he rested his heels on the hitching rail, hat tipped forward so that his eyes were shaded from the searing heat. A casual observer would have simply seen a man enjoying a doze in the sun. Closer observers, however, would have noticed that his hat had been carefully angled to ensure that there was a tiny space through which his open, alert eyes surveyed the street. They would also have noticed that his hands, lying loosely on his stomach, were rested inches away from the twin Colts which nestled in his well-oiled holsters. Even closer inspection would have led to the discovery of a badge with the inscription *US Marshal*, the tip of which poked out of Reuben's waistcoat pocket.

The hot sun was having its usual effect on the folk of Blanca Creek. Most had retired to a shady place or to the

16

saloon. There was little movement. An old man was sweeping the walkway outside the general store and a boy, about ten years of age, was splashing his face and neck in the horse drinking trough. Apart from that there was no life. No life, that is, until a group of men came riding slowly into town. Reuben's eyes fixed on them. He had seen them leave town early that morning accompanied by two others and he knew them from the posters he had seen in the sheriff's office in Flintlock. Shep Cassidy, Crazy Pete Robinson, and the Gambles twins were chatting quietly, each of them scanning the street with alert eyes.

Reuben's hands inched towards his firearms. As he watched, two more men joined them, riding out from the side street next to the livery stables. He recognized a man on a black and white pony as John Bridge, a suspected bank robber wanted in three states. Reuben didn't recognize the other man, a skinny, unkempt looking character in a green shirt. The men looked up and down the street as if they were assessing the situation, then they rode slowly in the direction of the county bank. The man in the green shirt and Jed Gambles stayed on their horses but the others dismounted and entered the bank, leaving their companions to hold the other horses and look for any signs of danger. After a few seconds, John Bridge emerged from the bank and said something to the green shirted man. Then hell broke loose. First, three shots from within the bank, immediately followed by John Bridge leaping onto his horse. Reuben Kane was on his feet in a split second and as he rose, he drew his guns in one lithe movement. Bridges turned towards him, recognizing him immediately. Both Bridges and the man in green went for their guns but they were way too late. Kane's Colts were already in his hands and he was firing even as the two men reached for their own guns. The first bullet struck Bridges in the chest; the second inflicted a mortal head wound on the man in green. Bridges continued to grasp for his gun but a second shot to his chest catapulted him from his horse and he lay dying in the street.

Kane was about to open fire on the men emerging from the bank when the young boy, panicked by the gunfire, ran straight across his line of vision in an attempt to get to home and safety. The split second of delay gave the four-some a chance to open fire and Reuben dived for cover behind the horse trough as their guns spurted a deadly orange flame volley. Reuben's horse was tethered to the rail and almost in slow motion he saw it crumple and fall under the hail of bullets. He realized that they had shot the horse as a deliberate tactic to slow him down and he cursed himself for being so careless by leaving the poor animal so exposed. The four fleeing men lashed their horses into action and rode hell for leather down the street. Reuben could only empty his guns as a gesture, knowing that already they were out of range. He checked his horse but knew that she was dead. Cursing to himself, he dragged the saddle off and went to the livery stable. 'I'm Marshal Reuben Kane. I need a horse.' The old man in the stable looked up but continued raking straw as if he was oblivious to the drama in the main street.

'Now!' barked Reuben and chose the best looking horse. 'I'm taking this one. The government will pay.' The old man started to protest but realized it was futile. 'Where do I send. . . ?'

'Sheriff's office. John Miles'll sort it out. Where is Sheriff Miles?'

The livery man, at last grasping the seriousness of the situation, shook his head. 'Don't rightly know. Not seen him since Monday. Probably gone to his other office. He'll be in Flintlock I guess.'

So there was no chance of Miles raising a posse. Reuben considered the situation. Four of them. One of him. He weighed up the odds for a few seconds and urged the old man to hurry. Five minutes later he was following the trail left by the robbers. It soon became clear that they were retracing their tracks. They had spent time in the town only to take the bank and they were returning from whence they had come. That meant that they had almost certainly worked out an escape route which would be difficult to follow. After a relatively easy first part, where he tracked the trail in loose sand, he arrived at a wide stream after which the tracks disappeared. He looked for tell tale marks on the stones in the stream, which would indicate which way the men had ridden, but he found none, which suggested that they had had the foresight to wrap the hoofs of their horses in some sort of cloths before entering the stream.

Reuben cursed under his breath then decided, for no particular reason, to ride downstream, looking intently on the banks for any traces of emerging horses. After half an hour he decided that he had made the wrong choice and retraced his steps to where he had entered the stream and started the process all over again, but this time moving upstream. The blazing heat was taking its toll.

Another long half hour passed before he spied a patch of disturbed ground where a horse had obviously been ridden out of the water. For nearly two hours he trailed painstakingly over rocks and brush, often losing the trail and retracing his steps, until eventually he arrived at open land on which the hoofs had once again left easy to follow signals. He guessed that the outlaws had believed themselves to be safe when they passed this point and indeed there appeared to be no attempt to cover the trail now. He passed Roy Gregory's Lazy Gopher ranch and headed towards the Crooked M, which came into sight as the sun began to slip slowly down to the horizon. He was very hot and near to exhaustion. Reuben could see no sign of life from the ranch as he urged his tired horse on. He had not met either of the owners of the Crooked M, but he knew their names, Ed and Sal McIntyre – and he aimed to change his horse for a fresher beast and also to find out if they had seen any riders before darkness made following the trail impossible.

He urged the horse into a gallop, then as he approached the house he slowed to a trot. A sixth sense, finely honed through years of experience, told him that it was time for caution. It was possible that Cassidy had left a couple of men with rifles behind in the house to pick him off. He rode forward cautiously and his right hand drew his Winchester from its holster. As soon as he saw the dead horse lying still attached to the rig he dismounted and crouched behind a wooden post, remaining still and silent, rifle at the ready. He surveyed the area in the fading orange light and saw three bodies. Two he recognized immediately as members of the Cassidy bunch. The third, although he didn't know it, was rancher Ed McIntyre. Even from this distance he could see by the unnatural posture that Ed was dead. Reuben remained silent and motionless for several minutes then he crouched down and moved towards the body. He checked and as expected, found that the young rancher was dead. Looking up, he could neither see nor hear any sign of life from the ranch house and he was still acutely aware of his exposure to attack in this vulnerable position, even though he felt pretty certain that the gang had moved on.

He crouched even lower and moved crab wise towards the house. Removing his boots, he stepped silently on to the veranda porch. All was silent. He pressed his back to the wall, then after listening for a full minute and hearing nothing he spun round, kicked open the door, simultaneously flinging himself stomach down through the doorway, with his levelled gun in his hand. He lay there in the gloom, still and silent. His senses were taut and he was listening for any sound which might indicate that someone was in the house. At length he heard a low groan from the bedroom. It was a woman's voice but still fearing a trap, he approached with caution.

Sal McIntyre lay on the bedroom floor where the men had left her. Her top had been ripped, exposing a bruised left breast. Bruises and scratches also covered her legs and her face was purple on the right side where she had been savagely punched. Blood had congealed around her lip; she looked close to death. Reuben lifted her and gently placed her on the bed then went to find a damp cloth and some water. He returned and tenderly cleaned her and wiped away the blood, cursing the men who had done this thing. He wiped a dark stain of congealed blood from her nose and as he cleansed it and looked at the battered, possibly broken woman, he knew without any shadow of doubt who was responsible for this atrocity.

Reuben took a deep breath and his lips twitched involuntarily. 'Shep Cassidy!' he growled.

Reuben looked down at the still form again and tried not to think what she had been subjected to at the hands of Shep and his mob. Finally, he stood up and walked to the door. Standing outside the ranch house, he looked at the sky and made a promise to himself. 'This ain't just the law, Cassidy,' he hissed quietly, 'you've made it more personal than that, you bastard.' Then he returned to the bedside and continued his ministrations. At length, she was clean and sleeping. Reuben took a hip flask and some coffee from his saddle-bag and poured himself a whiskey. He sat quietly on the wooden veranda looking at the stars in the cloudless sky and feeling the heat of the whiskey hit his throat. Not for the first time, he marvelled that the world carried on, still peaceful and beautiful, regardless of the horrors of the day. Above him, silence and indescribable beauty. A few yards away, three corpses.

He stood up, still staring at the bright stars shimmering in the deep blue-black night, then his mind returned to the task in hand and he exhaled wearily, and walked over to where the bodies lay. He removed Ed's guns and found a wallet in his pocket. It contained a few dollars – which he was surprised Cassidy hadn't stolen – and a picture of he pretty young woman whose battered being lay in the ranch house. Automatically, as a mark of respect, he removed his hat. He didn't want the woman to see the murdered man, whose face and head were badly damaged by the bullets from Pete's gun, so he found a shovel, went out of the house and dug a grave for Ed McIntyre then laid him to rest near the gate. The other two he carried on horses and buried in shallow graves outside of the ranch fence. Then, postponing the chase for the moment, he returned to Sal's bedside and waited for her to regain consciousness.

It was six hours before she showed signs of life. She opened her eyes and asked for her husband before falling again into a deep sleep. Night turned into dawn and dawn into day and he went out with his Winchester and killed himself some food to supplement the rations and coffee in his saddle bag, then he settled down in the ranch again. It was frustrating to know that with every passing minute, the murderers were putting more distance between themselves and the lawman but Reuben had no option but to stay with Sal McIntyre, who still slept a deep and mercifully dreamless sleep. Dusk returned and he lit the oil lamp, poured himself a coffee, made himself a stew ... and waited. He had fallen asleep in the chair by the fire when the screaming started. He leapt up and rushed to her bedside. She was wailing piteously and although her eyes were open she didn't see. She scratched and punched when he tried to calm her. Beads of sweat stood out on her forehead and rivulets ran down her face and chest. The writhing turned to convulsions and Reuben believed that she was about to die. Massive tremors caused her to throw herself across the room and Reuben had to lift her back and press her shoulders to the bed to save her from harming herself. She fell back on to the pillow, writhing and staring at the ceiling, shaking violently and moaning, then, eventually, she lay back and was still. He pressed a damp cloth to her forehead to try and reduce her temperature and occasionally her eyes would open and she would stare at the ceiling with eyes sometimes full of pain and hate and sometimes blank and dead. Then the screaming started again and she flayed at the air. It was a considerable time before his soothing voice started to have any effect. Her screams lessened and eventually she subsided, mentally and physically exhausted. She fell asleep clinging on to him and without knowing it he sang a quiet lullaby he remembered from somewhere in his distant childhood. Her breathing became more even and slowly she loosened her tight grip. He sat with her throughout the night, occasionally dozing but always at her bedside, watching anxiously for any change. In the morning, about an hour after dawn when he was dozing, she opened her eyes and spoke in a calm, clear voice. 'Who are you? Where's Ed?'

He tried to sound normal but he couldn't meet her questioning gaze. 'My name's Reuben Kane, ma'am. Marshal Reuben Kane.'

'Where's Ed?' she repeated and he averted his eyes. She stared at him and eventually he met her gaze.

'I'm sorry, ma'am,' he said softly. 'I found a man outside. He'd been murdered.' He described Ed and handed her the wallet and photograph which he'd removed from the body. She looked at the items for some time without making a sound, and then she pressed the wallet to her lips. The memories of the dreadful events flooded back and Sal McIntyre sobbed uncontrollably.

# CHAPTER THREE

# THE BEGINNING

They sat facing each other over breakfast. Sal was drinking a mug of coffee and she frowned over the steaming liquid. 'Tell me everything. What happened afore you found me?'

Reluctantly, censoring some of the details, Reuben recalled the gruesome events and as he finished, he poured himself another coffee from the simmering pot. 'As soon as you're well enough to ride into town, Mrs McIntyre—' He was interrupted by the sound of horses approaching the ranch and he immediately strapped on his guns and picked up his Winchester, checking that it was loaded and ready for action. Sal's eyes widened with fear. 'Stay here, ma'am.' He looked cautiously out of the door and saw a well dressed man aged in his fifties on golden stallion.

'Ed!' the rider shouted. 'Sal! You there?' Reuben walked out and faced the horsemen, rifle levelled.

Before anyone could say or do anything, Sal's voice sounded behind Reuben. 'Roy!' she exclaimed. Reuben turned to see that she was standing in the doorway with her husband's Colt in her hand. 'Roy,' she repeated, but quietly this time, then she sank to her knees.

Five minutes later, a shocked Roy Gregory, owner of the Lazy Gopher ranch, listened in horror as Sal finished telling him the bare bones of what had transpired. The colour drained from his face and he looked at Reuben, then at the marshal's badge which lay on the table. 'And you were trailing the men who did this?' Reuben nodded. 'What are you aiming to do, Marshal?'

'Now that you're here, I'll leave Mrs McIntyre in your hands and I'll saddle up and get after those bast— sorry, m'am, those *murderers* and bring them back.'

'Well, I'll be only too glad to take Sal to the Gopher and I'll ask some of my men to keep an eye on this place till Sal's decided what she wants to do and—' Sal interrupted him. Her face had changed and was set and hard. When she spoke, her voice was deadly quiet and allowed for no argument.

'Thank you kindly, Roy. But I'm not staying. I'm going with the marshal.'

Roy opened his mouth to protest but Sal waved him aside. 'I would be pleased if you would keep an eye on my ranch while I'm away but whatever you say, I intend to hunt those bastards down or die in the trying.'

There was a long silence, and then Reuben spoke. 'These men are killers, ma'am. They are fast and accurate with their guns. They ain't amateurs.'

Sal fixed an unblinking stare on him, and then appeared to ponder his words for a few seconds before standing up and nodding in his direction.

'Come with me, Marshal.' She walked to the door and went outside, followed by Reuben and Roy. 'Give me one of your Colts.' It was an order rather than a request.

Reuben looked at her hesitantly.

'Why do you want a gun, ma'am?'

She ignored his question and instead looked around and picked up five stones and placed them on the fence. Reuben stood in silence watching her and she spoke without looking at him.

'I aim to get back into practice so I can blow their heads off'n their shoulders.' She spoke in a flat, matter of fact tone and held her hand out. Reuben handed her his Colt and she checked their balance in her hands then, so quickly that it seemed she hadn't even aimed, she fired five shots. The stones flew off the fence.

'I only put five up in case I missed one. I'm rusty,' she said with no trace of irony. Then she pointed at a small fragment of stone which had broken off one of her targets.

'Throw that in the air.'

'But. . . .'

'Just throw it.'

Reuben tossed the stone high into the air and as it began to arc downwards the gun barked and the stone shattered into even smaller fragments.

Reuben pursed his lips and sucked in air. Recognition dawned. 'Sally Seddon.' He smiled faintly. 'I knew I'd seen you somewhere before. I was at Dakota when you shot a cigar out of the mayor's mouth. Some shooting. You sure know how to use a Colt, ma'am.' He paused and looked at the ground and she knew as sure as day what he was going to say next. 'But shootin' at stones ain't the same as killing a man who's trying to kill you. That's a totally different kind of shooting. Totally. To kill a man you've got to know how his mind works and if it's someone like Blackeye you've got to sink to his level afore you meet up with him. You've got to abandon everything you think of as decent and just concentrate on killing him afore he kills you.'

A long silence ensued, then she handed the gun back to Reuben and looked unblinkingly into his eyes.

'I'm going after them, Marshal. I'll go with or without you. It's your choice. But I'm going after them.'

Reuben smiled a mirthless smile.

'I guess you are at that,' he said quietly. 'I guess you are at that.'

Without another word she went back into the ranch house and minutes later she emerged in jeans, a loose fitting blue shirt and a buckskin top.

'I'm going to saddle up. Roy's gonna take care of the ranch. Are we going together or am I going to kill them myself?'

'Which direction are you headed, ma'am?'

'Wherever their trail takes me.'

'We don't know where they've gone, ma'am. The trail will be cold.'

Sal was mounting her horse already.

'Only way they could've gone is a mile or so south of the Lazy Gopher and on towards Flintlock. Nowhere else to go. Flintlock is about twenty miles away and there's nothing else. When we get to there I'll ask. When you're as ugly as them you sure can't ride through a small place like Flintlock without someone noticing.'

Reuben nodded, accepting the irrefutable logic.

'Well, Marshal, are you coming?'

He looked up at the determined, unsmiling face.

'I'm coming, ma'am.'

And now *she* smiled a slight smile, which pulled at the cuts on her lip and made her wince.

'Glad to hear it, Marshal. And if we are travelling together I'd be obliged if you called me Sal or Mrs McIntyre.'

He nodded at her.

'OK, Sal. And I'm Reuben. I don't want my profession advertised. It can attract the wrong sort of attention.'

'OK, Reuben. Saddle up and let's be on our way.'

Roy Gregory stood outside the doorway and watched Reuben saddle his horse. Deep in his heart he knew that Sal was making a bad mistake. She was a novice taking on hardened expert killers, but he knew her well and saw that her mind was made up. He approached her and laid his hand on the neck of her horse.

'Take care, Sal.' That was all he said and she smiled in reply. As they approached the gate, she stopped and looked at her husband's grave and Reuben nodded. She dismounted and walked alone to the crude wooden cross and rested her right hand lightly on it.

'I've gotta go, Ed. If I don't sort this business I'll never be able to farm here. I'll be back, and when I am I'll make the Crooked M everything we dreamed it would be. Keep an eye out for me, Ed. I love you.'

Then they rode off towards Flintlock.

For the first hour or so they rode in silence. She was deep in thought and he was looking for any signs to indicate that Cassidy and his men had passed this way, even though he knew the passage of time would almost certainly have erased any evidence. The silence was broken at length by Sal.

'Do you know anything about these men?' she asked.

'Plenty,' he replied. 'I was first sent to find them after they murdered a bank clerk and a young boy about three months ago. The trail ran dry until an old prospector said he'd seen them heading towards Blanca Creek. Originally there were nine of them but arguments and bullets have whittled them down. Shep Cassidy is the undisputed leader. A giant of a man – sorry, ma'am,' he apologized, cursing himself for his stupid insensitivity, 'I guess you know that already. Cassidy was a soldier who fought fear-lessly, but something in him turned bad and he started causing more and more trouble, brawling and drinking. In the end he killed a corporal in an argument over a card game. It was, legally at least, a fair fight as they both had guns. But the corporal was just a kid and his holster was a cavalry type with the lock on, so the reality was that he had no chance. Anyway, Cassidy was tried and found not guilty of murder but he was more trouble than he was worth and the cavalry decided to get rid of him. He turned to looting and bank robbery after being dishonourably discharged and he was perfectly suited to his new career. He has a well earned name for being ruthless and sadistic and he's wanted in at least three states for robbery, rape and murder and a whole list of other offences. Uses one of the few Buntline Special copies because he reckons the advan-tage in range outweighs the speed of the draw you get with a Colt and he keeps a knife hidden down his right boot which he can throw as accurately as most men can fire a gun.'

He paused, allowing Sal to digest what he had said.

'Crazy Pete Robinson is the second in command. Sometimes called Pancho because he wears a sombrero. The story is that he killed a young woman cos she refused to dance with him and he was sentenced to hang, but he escaped from prison after knifing the guard. He went on a spree of violence and murder. Seemed to kill people just for the fun of it and ended up murdering a friend of mine – a deputy sheriff – last year. That's what he has in common with Cassidy. They both enjoy killin' and inflicting pain. They do it fer the hell of it.' He paused and glanced at Sal. He was trying to bring home to her just how dangerous and lacking in feelings these men were, but he had crossed over the line. 'Sorry, ma'am.'

'Nice boys,' she said quietly.

'Indeed, ma'am. Nice boys.'

They rode on in silence as the sun began to set. He could see that Sal was once again enveloped in thoughts which, like the sky, grew darker as they travelled.

Before darkness completely descended they made camp for the night adjacent to a small stream. They sat quietly next to their fire and Reuben cooked some bacon in an iron pan. The silence continued as they ate then they watched the fire as it died down, listening to it splutter and staring at the orange glow.

Sal had wanted to ride on through the night, her eagerness to catch the men overriding all other considerations, but Reuben, experienced over many years, insisted that they stop and rest for the sake of the horses as well as themselves.

'The other thing is we'll be riding in the dark, which

31

makes us pretty open to ambush.'

'They'll be well gone by now,' she replied tersely.

'Mebbe they will. But there's plenty more than Shep Cassidy who might be riding this trail and some of them would be only too pleased to relieve a couple of sitting targets of their valuables in the night.'

She reluctantly agreed to stop for the night on the promise from Reuben that they would resume at daybreak.

Reuben poked the fire with a stick, causing a small shower of sparks.

'Where did you learn to shoot?' he asked.

'My pa taught me at first. I was hardly able to hold a gun but he decided that being able to shoot was essential in a wild land like this, so that's how it started. Me and Pa used to travel a lot. He used to get jobs on ranches and other jobs like bar tending, but I guess mainly he was a gambling man. Anyway, I was kinda good at shooting and found I could hit almost anything I wanted to. When I was fifteen a travelling show came to whatever town we were in and they had a shooting contest. I won and they asked me to join. Reached a stage where I could outdraw and outshoot almost anybody. Of course, you saw what I could do at Dakota.'

'And do you think you could kill a man in cold blood?' Reuben raised the question again and looked searchingly at her face in the orange, flickering light.

'Some men, no. *Those* animals? Believe it, Marshal. I already accounted for two of them.' She was emphatic and as if to ensure the message was clear she threw the dregs of her coffee into the fire, causing it to hiss and splutter. When she looked at Reuben something in his expression

32

told her that he was unconvinced. She spoke slowly, enunciating every syllable.

'They mur-dered my – hus-band. They raped me. I'd happily shoot them as they slept, only I'd like to see them suffer first jest so they know why they are going to die.'

'If you do get a chance to kill them,' said Reuben. 'It may be when they *are* asleep. They won't fight fair like in a story. If you get a chance to shoot them in the back you take it. It may be your last chance. If you hesitate you'll end up dead. Most people are handicapped by having a streak of decency and they *do* hesitate. That's why they end up in a wooden suit and Cassidy and Robinson are alive. Forget revenge and any thoughts of ensuring they know what's happening – it'll only cloud your actions and slow you down. Your aim is to kill them or bring them back to hang.'

'I won't ask for a chance and I won't give them one. Those animals deserve to die.'

Reuben detected a tremor in her voice and he still had qualms about this woman accompanying him. She had too much hate, which could lead her into making the wrong decision at a crucial time. A wrong decision could cost her her life but a wrong decision by her could also cost him *his* life.

'Just shoot to kill. That's how it must be.' He spoke wearily – almost sadly. 'But remember, when you kill a man you change – forever. A part of you will die with them regardless of how bad they were. Remember that. That's how it is.'

'I'll remember. Now, time for bed.'

Reuben thought that his words had probably fallen on deaf ears and he turned away as she adjusted her clothes then crawled under her blanket. Five minutes later he was asleep.

Sal lay there, staring at the stars through blurry tear-stained eyes.

# CHAPTER FOUR

# JOHN MILES

They rode into Flintlock in blazing sunshine and under a clear light blue sky. Reuben climbed stiffly from his horse and looked up at Sal. It had been a gruelling ride.

'First stop is the sheriff's office. Sheriff John Miles. An old friend of mine.'

They hitched up their horses and entered the poky little room which served as a sheriff's office. The office was sparsely furnished with a desk and two plain wooden chairs. A door led off to the jail. At the other side of the desk on a revolving chair a man in his mid fifties was dozing. He was balding, slightly overweight and a double chin wobbled slightly as he snored. His feet were resting on the desk, the scars on the wooden surface bearing testament to the fact that his spurs had often rested in a similar position. Reuben slapped his feet.

'Miles, you old dog. Wake up. You've got female company!'

Sheriff Miles opened his eyes and after a moment

adjusting himself to being awake, his face broke into a broad grin and he leapt to his feet.

'Reuben! Reuben Kane! How the hell are you? I hear you're still in the law business. And who's this? Sure is a pretty young thing. How the hell did an ugly bum like you find her?'

Reuben looked embarrassed and surprised. Reuben *was* embarrassed and surprised and, truth be told, he still thought of Sal as the battered and bloodied woman on the bed and he had never even noticed if she was attractive. He coughed and stared at John Miles then explained the situation to the sheriff, who immediately looked suitable crestfallen.

'I'm sorry, ma'am. If I'd realized I. . . .'

'No need for apologies, Sheriff. You weren't to know. A woman can hardly complain when someone reckons she's handsome.' Miles's face broke into a relieved wide, open grin and already she liked him. They sat down around the desk.

'Coffee?' Miles, without waiting for a reply, poured thick, aromatic coffee from an elderly black jug which sat on an even older stove in the corner, kicking heat into the already sweltering room. As he poured the strong black liquid, he talked over his shoulder.

'What brings you here, Reuben?'

'I'm looking for some men.' Reuben placed wanted posters on the desk. Miles returned and set mugs of coffee down on the ring marked surface then studied the crumpled pictures. After a few seconds he shook his head. 'I'm afraid I can't help you. But I've bin away for weeks in Barlow Valley. The posters are probably there in the tray with the other paperwork. You know what I'm like with paperwork, Reuben.' He grinned sheepishly.

'One day that failure to do your paperwork is going to get you a bullet in the back, John. These men have been wanted for a good while. If'n you can't recognize men like these they'll have a head start and—'

'I know. I know. No need to tell me, Reuben. Anyways, I suggest you ask Baz Potter. He owns the only saloon in Flintlock and sees everyone who passes through cos the town store is in the same building. You staying to eat? They do good steak at Kate's place.'

'We'll see,' replied Reuben. 'Baz Potter first. C'mon, Sal.'

They walked slowly down the sidewalk and Sal noticed that Reuben was watching from side to side and taking everything in. When they reached the swing doors of the saloon he stopped outside and looked over the door top. The saloon was empty apart from two cowboys playing poker and a short, bald barman in a striped shirt wiping glasses with a red and white check towel. He nodded to Sal and they both walked across to the bar. Sal was aware that the two cowboys and the barman were appraising her and she blushed slightly as she and Reuben leaned on the bar.

'Baz Potter?' Reuben asked.

'The same. And you are?'

'Reuben Blake. *Marshal* Reuben Blake.'

'And the lady?' Potter nodded in Sal's direction. 'We don't get many ladies in here.'

'Deputy Marshal Sal McIntyre.'

Sal didn't display any surprise at being introduced as a deputy but Potter's eyebrows rose slightly, although he said nothing as Reuben took the posters from his pocket.

'Have you seen these men, Mr Potter?'

Potter appraised the posters and showed no sign of recognition until he saw the pictures of Shep and Crazy Pete. He prodded them with a stubby finger.

'These two. Definitely. Day afore yesterday. The weasel one got drunk and hit one of the girls. Then they left and I heard they stayed in rooms at the house owned by Rachel Horne – 'Squirrel' Horne everyone calls her, but I don't know why. She lives in the white house just down the street next to the livery stables.' He paused expectantly. 'Now, are you just here to pump me for free information or are you buying a drink before you go?'

Reuben looked at Sal and she nodded and smiled.

'Whiskey,' she said. 'Two.'

Potter looked at her quizzically. It was unheard of for a woman to order a whiskey in his saloon except for the women who worked there, persuading visiting cowboys to part company with their wages.

'Two,' she repeated the word in an emphatic manner and Potter, not being a man to allow any chance of gaining money to slip through his fingers, nodded and placed a bottle on the bar then removed the cork.

Reuben was about to ask how she knew he wanted whiskey but decided to stay quiet. They leaned on the bar and both of them downed the drinks in one and poured two more. Reuben looked at the young woman and for the first time she smiled openly at him.

'Cheers, Mrs McIntyre. Let's drink to hunting down those prairie wolves and bringing them to justice.'

Sal's smile disappeared and she stared at the bar.

'I thought I told you already. I ain't intending to bring them anywhere, Marshal, 'cept mebbe in a wooden box. I intend to dispense justice without the expenditure of a trial.' She tapped the Colt on her hip as if to emphasize the point. 'That's the justice they deserve and, if I'm spared, then that's the justice they'll get.'

They stared at each other for a full five seconds, neither smiling nor blinking. Reuben, as a lawman, should have made some point about the necessity of law and the fairness of a trial. Instead, he smiled a wry smile.

'I guess if I'm truthful, that's what I had in mind too, Mrs McIntyre.'

'I think it's time to visit Rachel Horne, Marshal.'

'I think you're right, Mrs McIntyre.'

'Let's go, Marshal. And stop calling me Mrs McIntyre.'

Rachel 'Squirrel' Horne was a busy, precise little woman in her sixties, or maybe even seventies, with thick grey hair cut for convenience rather than style and gold rimmed glasses perched on her nose. Her appearance immediately illustrated to Reuben why she was nicknamed 'Squirrel'. She was immaculately neat and her skin shone from regular, scrupulous washing. Her grey hair poked up in bushy abundance and her black, darting eyes seemed to be looking for every movement around her. When she spoke it was in precise, clipped tones with a faint trace of a Scottish accent. Her movements, like her speech, were rapid and jerky.

'Come in, ye both!' Her invitation to enter her house sounded more like an order and the interior reflected her in its neatness and cleanliness. 'Now what can I be doing for you?'

'Marshal Reuben Kane, ma'am. I'm looking fer some men who we believe were involved in bank robbery and murder.' He studied Rachel's face to see if there was any reaction but there was none. When Reuben showed her the posters she recalled Shep and Pete with a sour frown.

'They booked rooms to stay here but after they'd eaten they went to the saloon and when they came back they were both drunk. Then this one joined them.' She pointed to the picture of Jed Gambles. 'I tried to tell them they weren't welcome in that state but the fat one pushed me aside. Knocked me clean over. He was sick on the stairs. Fat pig. The other one – he was wearing a sombrero – swore at me and called me names that I won't repeat.'

Reuben nodded. He could well imagine this spirited little woman challenging the two violent men and his face was wreathed in a broad grin.

'Is there something that amuses you, Mr Kane?' She pursed her mouth and glared at him and this time it was Sal McIntyre's turn to smile. Reuben stared hard at the carpet and looked contrite.

'Shep Cassidy, Jed Gambles, Shorty Gambles and Pete Robinson, ma'am.' Reuben spoke quickly before Rachel could take further offence. 'All of them violent men. Killers. The thought of you challenging them . . . well. . . .' He shrugged and smiled again and this time she saw the funny side and she uttered a short high pitched chuckle.

'I can see where you are coming from, Marshal. I suppose it must have looked pretty funny. Anyway, what do you want to know?'

'Did they say where they were headed, ma'am?'

'Nope,' she said without hesitation. 'But the man in the sombrero rode out. Said he was going south. He must have been heading to Wildcat Valley – that's the nearest town in that direction and about half a day's ride.'

'And Cassidy and Gambles?'

'Well now. I can be more precise about them. They only left me about five minutes ago after arguing over the bill. I wanted to charge them extra for the cleaning after the business on the stairs and the fat one became. . . .'

'Sorry, ma'am. Tell us that later, but now I need to know where they were heading.'

'Easy. They're in the place over the road – at Kate's place. Only good eating place in town.'

Sal left the room before Rachel Horne had even finished the sentence. Reuben turned and strode after her. She had already primed her Winchester by the time she reached the walkway outside the café and he grabbed her arm and held it in a vice like grip.

'Hold on there, Sal.'

She turned to him, her eyes round with anger.

'Hold on? Why? I aim to blast those sons of bitches to hell before they even know I'm here. You said not to give them a chance and surprise is the best weapon.'

Reuben kept his tight grip and nodded.

'I did so. I did so. But what if you burst in there and there are other people – maybe children – in the line of fire? What then? Do you open up and risk killing them? Cos what I do know is that Cassidy and Gambles won't think twice about gunning a few women and children down. They wouldn't even hesitate if it gave them an advantage.'

Sal ground her teeth and stared at the floor. She realized how stupid and headstrong she had been and she was silent for a few seconds. She looked up at Reuben.

'What do you suggest we should do?'

He loosened his grip and drew his Colt, checking that it was loaded even though he knew that it was.

'We wait. We wait till they come out. I'll stand in the street and you kneel behind those barrels and keep that rifle steady on the door. When they come out, as soon as one of them makes a move for his gun you shoot Jed Gambles. I'll deal with Cassidy.'

She hesitated, as if unsure of the wisdom of his plan, and then she nodded.

'OK. But . . . be careful, Marshal.'

'I specialize in being careful. You could even say it's my trademark. Now get yourself behind those barrels. And don't forget to keep an eye open fer any others who might be around.' Sal knelt behind the barrels and repeatedly checked her Winchester. Reuben had walked slowly to the middle of the street, facing the diner's door and she thought he looked vulnerable, but she could see that he was both relaxed and alert as he examined both his pistols and stood, loose limbed, before looking up and down the street searching for anything or anyone who looked suspicious.

He was concerned that innocent people might get hurt as no one was aware of the impending conflict and the few people around were casually going about their daily business. A boy, aged about twelve, was walking up the street playing with a toy wooden gun and Reuben called him over.

'What's your name, son?'

'James. James Davies, sir.' The boy looked at Reuben's badge of office. 'Say, are you a marshal, mister?'

'Yup. Marshal Reuben Kane. And I'm on the trail of some real bad guys and I need your help. Will you do something for me?'

The boy looked up expectantly at Reuben with wide eyes.

42

'Sure, Marshal. You name it.'

'Thanks, James. Now listen carefully. I want you to go over to Sheriff Miles's office and tell him that Marshal Kane is in the street and Shep Cassidy and Jed Gambles are in Kate's. Then when you've told him, you get back home as quick as your legs'll carry you. Do you understand?'

The boy's eyes were alight with excitement and he nodded gravely then turned and ran towards the sheriff's office.

Reuben reverted to his stance, facing the door of the diner. Sal kept the Winchester trained on the doorway and they waited.

After a few seconds the door opened and Shep appeared, followed by Jed. The men had obviously enjoyed their meal and a few drinks, and they were laughing and talking loudly. Neither of them saw Reuben, who was cursing the fact that John Miles hadn't arrived. He drew both of his guns.

'Cassidy! Gambles! Raise your hands high above your heads and keep them where I can see them!'

Jed Gambles complied immediately but Shep Cassidy reached for his long barrelled pistol. The length of the barrel didn't lend itself to a fast draw and he was further hindered by the fact that he had the gun thrust into his belt instead of a swivel holster. Sal McIntyre, crouched behind the barrels, saw the big man and she was blinded by hatred. She forgot her promise to aim for Gambles and instead she swung the barrel and fired, too quickly, at Shep Cassidy. Shep was still grasping for his gun when Sal found her mark with her Winchester and a red patch appeared on the left arm of his shirt. It was just a flesh wound but it angered the big man, who roared like a wounded lion. Reuben, who had already trained his gun on Cassidy, realized that Sal's desire for revenge had caused her to shoot at him, rather than at Gambles. Reuben, turning his gun on Jed Gambles, had lost a priceless split second. Gambles, taking advantage of the delay, lowered his hands, drew his gun and fired a wild volley at Reuben. The bullets flew harmlessly, digging holes in the ground some two feet in front of the marshal. Reuben's Colt flashed and a wet red gash appeared in Jed Gambles' stomach and he pitched backwards through the glass door of Kate's Eatery, shattering it into a thousand wickedly sharp shards.

Sal realized the enormity of her decision to gun for Cassidy instead of Gambles. She crouched down, watching the action as if she was a casual observer. In fact, she was frozen to the spot.

In the heat of the action, she didn't notice a figure in the shadows of the walkway behind Reuben. When she turned and recognized Shorty Gambles she tried to cry out to warn the marshal but no words came. She attempted to fire her Winchester but her body didn't respond and all she could do was to continue to watch the unfolding drama in frozen horror.

Reuben wondered fleetingly why a smile had suddenly appeared on Shep Cassidy's scarred face, then he was hit with the sudden realization that someone was standing behind him. He knew that it was Shorty Gambles. He knew that he was too late to outdraw him.

Shorty had levelled a shotgun at close range behind Reuben. Shep Cassidy, observing the momentary hesitation in Reuben's face, grinned maliciously and aimed his pistol. Then his expression turned to puzzlement as the blast rang out. Having seen Shorty aim his shotgun at such close range, he expected to see Kane pitch forward into the dust. Instead, Shorty took off backwards into the air, one hand clutching at a wound in his chest and his shotgun spinning harmlessly to the dusty street.

Shep took advantage of the hiatus. The only thought in his mind was survival and he swung back through the broken door of the diner, calling for Jed to join him in flight. The cut and bloodied figure of Jed Gambles rose, like a monster from the glass shard wreckage of the door. Jed started to shout his brother's name and then, swaying and dripping blood, he aimed at Reuben Kane. Too late. The guns in Reuben's hands barked and two bullets hit Jed just above his heart, separated by barely an inch. He spun on his heels in a crazy dance and ended facing the smashed door of the diner, a look of shock and incomprehension on his face. With a final, supreme effort, he tried to turn and face his assailant but his gun hung limply in his hand as he took one step forward before falling heavily face down into the street.

Jed Gambles and his brother were dead. Shep Cassidy fled through the café. In the yard at the rear he stole the nearest horse and within seconds he was riding hard out of town. Reuben Kane checked that no life remained in either of the Gambles twins and lit a cigarette before walking over to Sal, who was crouched behind the barrels. Her Winchester was still aimed at where Shep and Jed had been standing.

'Sal?' She looked up with shocked, glazed eyes and she was vaguely surprised to see the concerned face of Reuben Kane looking down at her. 'Sal, I guess I owe you my life.

You took Shorty Gambles out before he could shoot. Saved my skin. I owe you.'

Sal didn't reply. She still held the gun in a vicelike grip and stared at the bodies in the diner doorway. She was vaguely aware of John Miles tipping his hat back on his head. The distant voice of Baz Potter sounded.

'You're thanking the wrong person, Reuben. It was John Miles who shot Shorty.'

'Saw the bastard creep up on you and gave him both barrels of old Betsy here,' said Miles, tapping his shotgun with a wry smile. 'Mrs McIntyre couldn't see him there.'

As John Miles spoke Sal noticed a shadow in the alley next to the saloon. Instinct told her that something was wrong and she stared past the two men, trying to focus on the shadow. There was an orange flash and the dull thud of a slug making contact with human flesh and bone.

Reuben and John turned as one but the shadow had gone and all they could hear was the sound of a horse galloping full tilt out of town. Then Reuben slowly toppled forward on to his knees, his hand clutching a scarlet stain on his shirt.

Sal stared at him, horrified and hypnotized by the sight. *She* was facing the alley. *She* should have seen what was happening in the shadows and warned him. She moved towards him and put her hand on his cheek.

She had let him down badly by ignoring his orders and by failing to warn him of danger.

Now maybe she had cost him his life.

# CHAPTER FIVE

# THE FIND

John Miles looked down at his friend then turned to Sal McIntyre. He wore a sad, tired smile as he put his arm around her slim shoulders. The doctor ran across the street and he knelt next to Reuben, made a quick examination and beckoned to a couple of onlookers, who walked towards him.

'Get him into my surgery. Quick. I need to see if they hit anything vital.'

John held Sal close to him. The events of the past few days and the violence of the last few minutes had finally caught up with her and she sobbed uncontrollably as they carried Reuben to the surgery. Miles looked into the face of the young woman, still bruised and scarred from her treatment at the hands of the Cassidy mob, and he felt her sobs racking her body.

'It was my fault, John. If I'd acted, he would still be. . . .'

'You mustn't think like that, Sal. Not ever. There's no point in casting blame. When you're dealing with the likes of Cassidy you have to make split second life or death deci-sions. We all know the risk an' sometimes we make a wrong call. Reuben knew the risk – and he thought it was worth taking.'

'But it was *still* my fault. And the others have gotten away – including that bastard Cassidy.'

They made their sombre way to the surgery and sat outside as the doctor made his examination. After ten minutes he poked his head round the door and smiled.

'Good news. Just a deep flesh wound. He'll be out of action for a while. Bed rest is what I recommend, but he'll be fine in a couple of weeks. Tough as a pair of old boots.'

Sal sat next to the bed, a wave of relief passing through her body. She gripped Reuben's hand and smiled. 'I'm sorry, Reuben. It was all my . . .'

'Sshhh, Sal. Nobody's fault. These things . . .' He paused for breath. 'These things happen. Lawman's lot.' John Miles grinned at Reuben.

'You lump of sh-stone. Why, I reckon the whole of the Cassidy gang could aim at you and you'd still end up with jest a nick. Still, you ain't going to be chasin' no one for a while yet. You gotta stay in bed. Doc's orders.'

But his words were wasted as Reuben had fallen into a deep sleep induced by the drugs administered by the doctor.

'Now, Sal. You mustn't blame yourself. There's nothing we can do. Reuben's out of the game and they're headed out of my jurisdiction and I can't follow. But they'll come back sooner or later and I'll round up a posse and I'll bring them back, dead or alive. I promise you that.'

Sal looked up at him. Her expression had changed and her relieved smile had disappeared like the morning mist and been replaced by an expression which chilled him. Her eyes were as cold as clay. She spoke, very slowly, as if she was deliberating over every syllable.

'They might have left your territory, Sheriff, but they've not left mine. There's no reason why *I* can't go after them.'

'Now listen, Sal. You're upset. That's natural. But . . .'

'No, Sheriff. You listen. Am I or am I not a deputy marshal, appointed legally by Reuben Kane?'

'We-ll, I guess. But . . .'

'No "buts", Sheriff. As I say, they're still in *my* territory. I'm on my way. The colder the trail gets, the less chance I have of catching them. I've let Reuben down and I owe it to him and now I'm going to track them bastards and bring them to justice – kill them or be killed myself in the attempt.'

He looked at her, full of misgivings.

'Mrs McIntyre, they are experienced, professional killers. They don't think the same as normal people. They'll kill you, or worse, without any hesitation or remorse.'

'John. Reuben told me all of this already and as to them killing me or worse – well, they've done their worst already and I'm still here. I'm sorry, John. It's something I've got to do, for Reuben and for me, but mainly for my husband Ed. They murdered him and left him to the vultures just for fun. I won't be able to rest till I even the score so I can go back to the Crooked M and lay flowers on my husband's grave.' Sheriff Miles put up token resistance but it was futile.

'OK, Deputy. But don't go tonight. It'll be dark and dangerous. It's downright stupid to trail men like that at night. They're. . . .'

'I know. I know. I told you, Reuben already lectured me about that too. So when?'

'You come over to my place. Eve will make you something to eat. We'll sleep and rise early with fresh horses and supplies.'

Sal nodded demurely. She suddenly felt totally exhausted and realized that unless she found somewhere to sleep she would be good for nothing.

'Yes, Sheriff,' she said meekly.


Eve Miles was a female version of John. She was slightly plump, with a face given to ready smiles. She was horrified at the sight of Sal's battered face and she fussed over her like a mother hen, repeatedly persuading her not to go in search of the killers but eventually giving up, realizing, like John Miles and Reuben Kane before her that Sal was not to be moved. Sal was still convinced that she wouldn't be able to eat but the smell of home cooking drifting in from the kitchen made her salivate and they ate enormous portions of homemade stew before retiring to bed early. Sal slept fitfully, waking at one point to find Eve Miles sitting next to her bed.

'You were crying out, my dear,' said the woman, stroking Sal's perspiration soaked forehead. And with the comfort of the mother figure beside her, Sal fell again into a restless, dream filled sleep.

It was still not light when Eve Miles shook her gently by the shoulders.

'Time to get up, my dear. And I thought you might need these. Baz Potter brought them over.' Inside a brown paper package were clothes more suited to riding than the

ones Sal wore. A buckskin shirt and hard wearing leg pro-
tecting leather trousers.

'Will they fit?' asked Sal.

'Knowing Baz Potter's eye for the ladies, they'll fit all
right. He's provided every woman in town with their
outfits for more years than he cares to remember.'

The smell of griddled bacon and eggs was already per-
meating the air and even after the meal which she'd eaten
only a few hours ago, Sal enjoyed her breakfast.

'C'mon, Deputy McIntyre. Let's get you saddled up.' It
was John, wiping his hands and taking one last sip of
coffee before kissing his wife.

Eve turned to Sal.

'Take care, my dear. And come back to us soon.'

The two women hugged tightly and then Sal, afraid that
the tears might begin to flow, pulled away, left the house
and mounted her horse. John Miles patted the animal's
neck.

'Remember. Don't give them an even chance. There's
at least two or three of them – probably more – and they
are good at killing. I know you've already heard it, but
killing's what they do best. If you see them, even if they
have their backs to you, shoot first and ask questions later.'

'Thanks, John. I'll bear that in mind.'

'God speed, Sal. Go safe.'

John's words sounded fatherly. She felt deeply moved
by his concern and she leaned down and kissed him lightly
on the forehead before flicking the horse into action
before he could see her sad tears.

She rode quickly into the cool morning, deep in
thought as she covered the lonely dusty trail. Her thoughts
whirled round – thoughts of Ed, Reuben and the kindness

51

of John and Eve Miles and the unexpected generous gift from the tiny womaniser, Baz Potter.

A large part of her wanted to turn back and return to the Crooked M, to the life she had known before Shep Cassidy had ridden in. But would it be possible without Ed? Would she ever be able to settle down without avenging the crimes against her and her husband? Sal knew, beyond any doubt, that her life was changed forever.

She approached a rise and stopped at the crest and wiped her forehead. Stretching below her lay a tree clad deep, long valley, at the base of which rolled a fast flowing river. Silently, she surveyed the scene and breathed in the chill, sweet morning air. It was stunning. The purples and blues of the morning complemented the distant roar of the current as the water tumbled over the smoothed rocks. But she didn't take in the beauty. For Sal McIntyre, the valley was simply another obstacle between her and her quarry. At first, she had been seeking revenge for her husband, now she was aiming to avenge Ed and Reuben Kane. By dispensing rough justice, she believed that she would save others from the suffering which she was going through. She also believed that when she finally dealt with them, she, if not Ed and Reuben, could find some sort of peace.

Her thirst for justice, or maybe revenge, was tempered with guilt. This was a feeling which had been growing since the shooting of Reuben Blake. She knew deep in her heart that Reuben could so easily have been killed and for that she blamed herself. She nudged her horse gently down the steep and crumbly slope and she renewed her vows to herself to gain justice for Reuben, but a small voice in her mind asked if she wanted justice or revenge. As the slope levelled out she brought her heels sharply to its side and kicked it into a gallop. She decided that, justice or revenge, whichever it was, it didn't matter.

'I'll get you bastards!' she shouted out loud to herself. 'So help me, I'll get you!'

Eventually she reached the banks of the river and dismounted to let the horse drink. The water was icy cold and she splashed her face and neck then sat on a large rock, deep in thought and listening to the mellowing sound of the water. After some time, she moved, took off the buckskin jacket and drenched herself and her grubby shirt with the cooling liquid.

'Well, I'll be. . . .' The voice seemed to come from nowhere and shocked Sal, who had believed that she was alone. She spun round and grabbed for her jacket which lay next to her gun belt atop the rock. As she did so a shot rang out from the gun which had appeared in the hand of the rider. A bullet ricocheted off the rock, barely two inches from her hand, causing her to jump back in alarm.

There were two men, both skinny, both smiling and relaxed in the knowledge that they had surprised the apparently defenceless woman. The taller of the two stared down at Sal.

'Now then, ma'am. You shore are a sight fer sore, tired eyes. Now don't you go glarin' at me so unfriendly like. How about a bit of neighbourly friendship? What do you think, Johnny?'

'Well, I believe you are being mighty unfriendly, ma'am.'

'I agree, Rab. Mighty unfriendly. And you wouldn't want to upset us now, would you, ma'am?' And he smiled a mirthless smile, showing gapped and yellow teeth. 'Now stand up straight so the dog can see the rabbit.'

Memories of her treatment at the hands of Shep Cassidy flashed through her brain. For a moment Sal panicked and wanted to cry out, to beg for mercy – anything to stop these two animals. Then she remembered the words of Reuben Kane. The advice to remain calm and measured. She regained her composure, despite being in such a vulnerable position.

She cursed herself for being stupid enough to have stayed so near to the woodland, making it so easy for them to have cover on their approach. She gritted her teeth and tried to think of a way to turn the tables.

The man called Johnny had dismounted and he walked slowly towards her, a lascivious grin spreading over his face. His companion holding the gun, who still remained on his horse, spat some chewing tobacco and spoke in a slow drawl.

'Ah think you ought to persuade the little lady to be a mite more friendly, brother.'

Johnny raised his hand and growled. 'Do as I say, woman, and we *might* decide not to kill you.'

'Now Johnny, that ain't no way to go about it. What she needs is a gentleman.'

His companion, however, was in no mood to hesitate.

'Get down, you bitch!' he spat, and as the other man began to dismount, Sal saw her chance.

'Sure, Mr Johnny.' She tried to smile and look deferential. Inside she was sick with fear. She sat down and he walked towards her, smiling arrogantly. Such was his confidence that he hardly noticed her hand move towards the rock and when he did begin to understand, his realization was too late and she twisted like a snake and suddenly a

54

gun was in her hand and he saw an orange flash then felt a searing pain just below his ribcage. He was flung back by the impact and groaned in pain. The other man was still dismounting and had one foot in the stirrup as he swung himself over his mount. The horse, frightened by the gunfire, reared on its hind legs then shot forward, causing Rab Davies to fall backwards and land heavily on his back on the rocky ground. His pistol flew out of his grasp and clattered along the stony surface. Sal aimed her Colt with slow deliberation and shot him. She had aimed for the chest but his sudden movement resulted in her bullet tearing into his shoulder, causing him to scream out. She turned to the other man, who was lying on his back jerking occasionally and, she guessed, close to death. With total coolness born of anger, she stepped over to where the other man lay. She levelled the Colt, and then pointed it at his crotch.

'So I'm guessing that if him over there is Johnny, and you're Rab, then you're the Davies Brothers.'

He nodded, uncomprehending.

'. . . and you rode with Shep Cassidy?'

He nodded again. This time there was fear and slyness mingled with the lack of comprehension. He tried to return her unblinking stare but his hand began to move towards his gun.

'Don't even try, you bastard. If you do, I'll shoot your knees and hands and leave you here to die.'

'Who the hell—'

'Shut your mouth!' she snapped and stood over him, her feet either side of his shoulders. 'Y'know, you sure are scum, Rab Davies. I can smell you from here. Or is that just fear?'

Rab started to wriggle with the pain from his shoulder. She wished that she could finish him off and the advice of Reuben and John Miles echoed in her mind but she knew that she couldn't kill a helpless human being in cold blood, even one as loathsome as Rab Davies.

'Stay still!' she barked. 'You move, breathe and speak when I tell you . . . and only then. Do you understand?'

He looked up at her uncomprehendingly. How did this woman know his name? What did she want with him?

'Quite a coincidence. Meeting you of all people out here in the middle of nowhere.'

'Where. . . ?' he gasped through the pain.

'You don't recognize me, do you? But I guess murder and rape are pretty unimportant to scum like you. Let me help you remember. Do you recall a ranch where you killed the rancher? The Crooked M? Then you took his wife. You an' Cassidy and the others. Are you beginning to remember now?'

Behind her, Johnny Davies made a low gurgling sound and she turned momentarily. Rab saw his chance and grabbed her leg with his good arm and pulled. He grinned as she fell forward and such was his belief that she was helpless that he didn't see her bring the gun down in a savage arc. He heard his own nose splinter and then she was up, gun in hand and standing over him again.

'Bad move, Davies. Bad, bad move.' Involuntarily he grabbed again at her leg and earned himself a savage kick in the mouth.

'So now you've got what you wanted, Davies. We're close and personal.' She laughed a hollow laugh. 'But I guess you didn't quite picture it like this, huh?' She traced her gun lightly around his face. In the back of her mind a voice told her that she had gone beyond any boundary of decency and that she should stop, but the ache caused by her lust for revenge overcame every other emotion. What she intended to do next she didn't know but whatever her plans might have been they were changed in an instant as she saw Rab turn his eyes in the direction of his brother.

Johnny Davies, with a superhuman effort, had dragged himself to where his gun lay and as she turned he was raising it to aim at her back. She spun round and her gun barked twice and he jerked backwards, clearly dead before his head hit the ground.

Finding strength born of fear, Rab grabbed for Sal's gun. He crushed her fingers and the gun exploded, the bullet flying harmlessly into the air. Even with, or possibly because of his wounds, Rab found strength enough to throw Sal from him and as she fell he twisted the gun from her grasp and suddenly she found herself lying on her side, looking down the barrel of her own Colt .45.

Davies lay on his side, pointing the gun at Sal's head. Then he laughed mirthlessly.

He nodded at his brother's body, shook his head and muttered under his breath. Then he threw back his head, stared at Sal and laughed again.

# CHAPTER SIX

# THE TURNING

Rab Davies grinned savagely, displaying broken teeth and blood. This woman was going to pay and pay dearly for what she had done to him and Johnny.

'Now, you murdering little witch. Now you are going to feel scared in a way you never felt scared before.' He motioned for her to come closer. Confident now, he snapped out an order, causing himself some pain from his mouth wounds which only increased his desire to make her suffer. 'Move! I want to see you beg for mercy.'

Sal stared up at him.

Rab couldn't understand why there was no trace of fear in her eyes as she raised herself almost casually and walked towards her horse.

'Stand still or I'll blast you to hell, you murdering bitch!'

She stopped and turned, then to his amazement she smiled sweetly.

'You're going to blast me to hell, Rab? I don't think so.

Not with *that* gun.' She paused, watching his puzzled expression and savouring the moment. She hissed rather than spoke.

'Not with that *empty* gun.'

She smiled again and nodded towards the pistol. His expression changed from cruel arrogance, first to doubt then to defeat.

'Six bullets. Six shots, Rab,' Sal continued in a relaxed, mellow voice. 'And you sure ain't fit enough to reload it afore I get my Winchester from my saddle-bag.'

The truth was that Sal wasn't at all sure what to do next. She knew deep down that she couldn't gun Rab down in cold blood but no alternative plan of action came to mind. As things turned out it was Rab who made the decision for her.

He pulled the trigger, hoping against hope that Sal had not counted the number of shots correctly. He almost wept when he heard the click as the hammer fell harmlessly on the empty chamber. Frantically, stupidly, he reached for the bullets in his belt, slowed by the pain from his shoulder. He overcame the pain and reloaded one shell and raised the gun but even as he did, his eyes filled with terror and he knew he was too late.

Three explosions. Three shells from Sal's Winchester thudded into Rab. He landed heavily on his back then looked down and saw the neat, tight pattern on his chest which was rapidly becoming one large red stain. He stared at her as if surprised by her accuracy, then he sat up, vision blurred and body wavering. Rab fired one haywire shot from where he fell. It should have been harmless but it ricocheted off the hard rocky ground and a splinter of stone flashed at Sal, causing a flesh wound in her left thigh.

Another shot from Sal's Winchester and he was hit again in the chest. Any normal man would have been dead after the first volley, but with a superhuman effort driven by pure hatred, Rab Davies tried to haul himself to his feet. He almost reached a standing position but his legs buckled and he fell backwards into the river. Briefly he raised his head and stared at his killer, then he slid further into the water and his body was carried away by the current.

There followed a long silence, then Sal picked up her Colt and reloaded both it and the Winchester before picking up the weapons of the two brothers and stuffing them into her saddle bags along with their ammunition.

She felt totally calm and she mounted her horse slowly before looking at the body of Johnny. She never even felt the pain of her wound and she heard her own voice.

'Two more down. Job done. Time to go, Sal.'

She had ground to cover and she wanted to reach town before dark.

Sal arrived at Redwood as dusk began to fall. The large sinking sun turned the distant mountains a bright orange as she rode slowly down the main street.

She reflected just how life had changed in a few violent days. From being the contented wife of a rancher, she had become a vengeful killer. She had seen Reuben gunned down and witnessed the deaths of several men. She shuddered and stared skywards, perhaps at God. What was she becoming? What had she already become?

It was as if she was emerging from a trance. She became vaguely aware of a pain from her left leg and she looked down and saw a patch of blood which was still sticky.

John Miles had given her clear instructions that on her

arrival in the town she should go to the end of the street to the red house with the big garden, where his old friends Margy and Frank took in occasional guests. Sal dismounted outside the house and realized that she was totally exhausted. She leaned against the porch and knocked on the door. Frank, a small, nervous looking man answered. Sal was swaying slightly.

Seeing the patch of blood on Sal's leg, Frank immediately took her horse to the stable and his wife Margy set up a hot bath for Sal to bathe herself and clean her wound. Margy was the opposite of her husband. A large, smiling woman whose personality matched the size of her body.

Sal luxuriated in the hot bath. The bruises from her attack were fading but still visible and she cleaned the wound on her leg. It was only a minor flesh wound but it was quite painful and she winced as she dabbed at it with a clean damp cloth. She looked at the bruises on her legs and thighs and suddenly, without warning, tears started to cascade down her cheeks, mingling with the steaming bathwater. It was a cathartic release and she wept for a full ten minutes, after which she felt her muscles unwind as she sank deeper into the tub. The heat of the water began to eradicate the pain and for the first time since the murder of her husband, her body relaxed.

# CHAPTER SEVEN

## CASSIDY

Shep Cassidy and Pete Robinson sat at an elderly table in the Crazy Lady Saloon in Redwood. They had enjoyed a night with the saloon girls and consumed a fair amount of whiskey. Now they were relaxing with the remaining contents of the bottle.

'Strange thing,' Pete mused, staring at the bottle and wondering why it was nearly empty.

'Strange? What's strange?' enquired Shep, trying to focus through a whiskey induced haze.

'No Rab. No Johnny. They ain't turned up and we was supposed to meet up here. Unusual fer them, especially when there's money to be had.'

Shep shrugged his massive shoulders.

'Could be lotsa reasons. Horse gone lame, or mebbe they got lucky with a woman. Could be drunk. Could be shot.' He pointed two fingers in an imitation of a gun at Pete and laughed.

'I guess so. Still strange though. They's usually on time.'

At the same time as Shep and Crazy Pete were having their slurred conversation, Sal, a few hundred yards away and unaware of their proximity, was getting dressed, her face pink from the heat of the bath. She donned her shirt and pants but instead of the usual single Colt, she crossed two gun belts, the second being that which she had removed from Rab. She looked at the reflection of herself in the mirror with Colts on either hip. She had the Colts facing backwards – the trigger facing front. It was an unusual look and demanded a cross draw, left hand going for the gun on the right hip and right to the left. She smiled to herself. In the old days of the shows she had practised for hour upon hour and finally she had been able to cross draw and hit a moving target with as near as damn it a hundred per cent accuracy. She drew the guns on her reflection, flicked them backwards and replaced them in her holsters. She felt confident that she could still draw rapidly and hit her target. A knock on the door interrupted her.

'Come in!' she shouted and Frank entered. The little man bobbed nervously in the doorway and smiled.

'We'll be having supper in half an hour, Mrs McIntyre. Is that OK for you?'

'That's fine, Frank. But I've got a bit of business in town first. Shouldn't take long. Oh, and please call me Sal. Mrs McIntyre makes me feel old.'

'Why, you don't look old, Sal. You look mighty pretty and. . . .' His voice faded and he blushed like a schoolboy. 'Heck, I'm sorry. I didn't mean.'

'Don't apologize.' Sal laughed. 'It's good to have a compliment, especially after the last few days.'

He laughed too – a relieved chuckle, and then he

looked thoughtful and remained standing silently in the doorway, shifting his weight from one foot to the other. Sal was aware of his presence.

'Is there anything else, Frank?'

'We-ll. I sort of don't like to mention it, Mrs M— Sal, but walking the streets alone after dark ain't the sort of thing a lady does in Redwood. Hell! It's not the sort of thing *any* person with any sense would do in Redwood. We get some kinda rough characters passing through. Definitely not the place fer a lady.'

Sal smiled a dazzling smile and tightened her gun belt.

'Good job I ain't no lady then, Frank.' Then she was gone.

The street was still quiet as she walked to a building which bore a gold sign with ornate black lettering proclaiming it to be the Dawson Provisions Emporium – in reality a small shop opposite the saloon which didn't live up to the grandiose sign.

Inside, the shop was illuminated by two oil lamps. A tall, cadaverous looking man stood behind the counter, slightly stooped and peering myopically though a pair of thick-lensed spectacles.

'Evening, ma'am. Welcome to Redwood. John Dawson at your service.'

'Sally McIntyre. But call me Sal.'

He smiled a mournful smile at her and she reflected that he would be an excellent professional mourner. Then she purchased some ammunition and some candy and placed the money on the counter.

'Nice town you have here, Mr Dawson.'

'*Was* a nice town, Mrs McIntyre. *Was.*'

He peered over her shoulder through the window at

the saloon.

'We used to have a mighty fine community till Shep Cassidy and Pete Robinson rode into town last year.' He appeared not to notice Sal's expression of interest at the mention of the names. 'But now a lot of the decent folk have upped sticks and left. Since Cassidy and his boys arrived the town's started to die. Aw, we used to have the occasional fracas when drunken cowboys came off the trail but the sheriff would always sort it out and they'd cool down after a night in the cell.'

'And what happened?'

'Shep Cassidy and Pete Robinson happened. Everyone's scared of them and they run the town.'

'Don't you have any law here?'

Dawson laughed mirthlessly.

'We *did*. We had a sheriff but he was jest a local man who kept the peace when we had a quiet town. Shep threatened him one night in the Crazy Lady an' he handed in his star before dawn and hightailed it out of town. Never bin seen since.' He licked his lips and stared at Sal. 'Guess I cain't blame him.'

'Will you elect another sheriff?'

'We already have. And, on the face of it all above board and that. Trouble was that Shep Cassidy put forward his own man and . . . and he *persuaded* people to vote fer him.'

'Who did he appoint?'

'Jack Tucker. Rode with Cassidy some time back then went into hiding after an incident up country.'

'So there's no law in town?'

'Well, strictly speaking there is law of sorts. Basically, any person fool enough to rile any of Shep's boys is either beaten within an inch of their lives or. . . .' He looked around to ensure that no one was within earshot '. . . or they're shot at a time when Shep and all his boys have twenty witnesses who'll swear on the Bible that neither of them were in the neighbourhood.'

Sal leaned on the counter, trying to look in part shocked and in part disinterested. She knew for certain now that Cassidy and his clan were in town to stay. She also knew what Shep didn't know, namely that some key members of his gang were dead.

'I think I know some of the boys Cassidy rides with.' She named the dead men and looked up at Mr Dawson. 'Have I missed anyone out?' she asked artfully.

If John Dawson considered this a strange question he displayed nothing in his expression. Had it been a man asking the question he would have assumed that it was a gunman or a bounty hunter, but why this attractive young woman wanted to know was beyond him. He had noticed that she was wearing guns and he hesitated slightly before answering.

'We-ell.' He rubbed his chin thoughtfully. 'There's Sheriff Jack Tucker of course. Then there's Pete Robinson and Abe Coulson. There's a couple more, but they jest kinda make up the numbers and I need to think to remember any names.'

Abe Coulson! The mention of the name shocked Sal. She vividly remembered the day, all those years ago at her sharpshooter show when he had outdrawn her in a best of three competition. She turned away from Dawson and feigned interest in some cloth, giving herself time to regain her composure. After a few seconds she spoke as casually as she could, still looking down at the cloth.

'So do you plan to stay in town, Mr Dawson?'

'I'm too long in the tooth to start up again now. My wife's buried here and I've gotten my roots deep down. Anyways, who'd buy a store here with Cassidy running the town? I guess I'll jest keep my head down and carry on.'

'Don't you think the town could fight back?'

'Oh, we tried that, ma'am. We stood up agin them when they was electing the sheriff.'

'And. . . ?'

'John Mason, Sean Baverstock and Pete Mogg. All good men. All got nice markers on the slope.'

'The slope?'

'The graveyard, ma'am. Cassidy's boys gunned them down. Said they was resisting arrest. No witnesses.' He looked out of the window with expressionless eyes. 'Yes, ma'am, the Cassidy boys are good at killing. It'll take a special man to—'

He abruptly stopped speaking when the door opened and a tall, square jawed man strolled in. He was crisply dressed in what was clearly an expensive red shirt, leather waistcoat and well tailored black trousers. Sal noticed immediately that he wore twin pearl handled pistols slung low in leather holsters so that his hands naturally rested on the gun butts. On his chest was a silver star. He nodded at Sal and raised his Stetson. 'Ma'am. Welcome to our little town. I'm Sheriff Jack Tucker. I heard you'd rode into town and I like to know who's around. Kind of unusual, a woman riding alone. Especially in buckskins and carrying twin Colts. You here on business?'

Sal was impressed by his quick observations and she smiled at the sheriff.

'Indeed I *am* here on business, Sheriff. My husband ran off with a wildcat saloon girl and headed through Flintlock in this direction. I lost his trail about five miles from here. You obviously keep a close eye on things, Sheriff. Have you seen any sign of the cheating bastard? Tall man. 'Bout your height. Slim, with a droopy moustache. The whore is a brassy redhead with bad taste in clothes.'

Sal glanced at the two men and their expressions didn't indicate that they believed her story. Tucker struck a match on the doorpost, lit a cigarette and inhaled before speaking.

'Not seen *any* couples, ma'am. You're the first stranger this week 'cept fer the tall feller who rode through town today. Wondered if you might know who he is, being as how the both of you came on the same day.' He paused to see if there was any sign of a reaction in Sal's expression but there was none. 'He's tall, as I said and spare framed. Mebbe forty. Mebbe more. Wears his gun low, as if he's used to using it. Just seemed strange that we get two new-comers on the same day.' He paused, then stared at Dawson, who looked down at the counter and brushed off an imaginary speck of dust, then the sheriff fixed his unblinking stare on Sal. 'You see, I don't believe in coin-cidence, ma'am.'

Sal began to feel out of her depth. This man was no fool and she determined to end the conversation. She smiled brightly.

'Well, Sheriff, if you *do* see them, be sure to let me know. You sure as hell can't miss her, with her mass of hair and her clingy dresses.'

'Will do, ma'am. But my guess is that they've doubled back on themselves and headed back to Flintlock. Ain't nothing much past here for a good fifty miles 'ceptin' fer Ennerman.'

'Ennerman?'

'A ghost town these days. Last people left there five years and more ago. So unless you've got any business here in Redwood I'd advise you to turn around tomorrow and head back to Flintlock.'

'Thank you kindly for your advice, Sheriff Tucker. The ride's tired me out and I think I'll ask around to see if anyone's seen the lying bastard. Worst thing is he took $100 – my life savings – to spend on that whore. I'm damned if I'm going to let him get away with it. I want his hide hanging on the barn door.'

'I see your reasoning, ma'am. I'll be sure to let you know. What did you say his name was?'

'I didn't,' said Sal. She thought that maybe there were details of her husband's murder in the sheriff's office and Tucker might put two and two together when he got talking to Cassidy. She said the first name which entered her head. 'It was Carson. Ed Carson.'

Tucker looked her up and down, noticing the rounded curves underneath the buckskin. For the first time he smiled appreciatively.

'I'll be sure to keep a look out, Mrs Carson. Good luck. I hope you find him. He must be a mighty foolish man to give up a woman like you for a saloon girl.' He nodded at Sal and Dawson and left the shop.

John Dawson looked sideways at Sal and she recognized a cool shrewdness in his eyes which worried her. He rubbed his stubbly chin and paused as he made a decision.

'D'you mind if I give you some advice? Sort of advice for your good health?'

'Go ahead, Mr Dawson.' Sal's voice betrayed uncertainty and she pursed her lips.

'It seems a bit strange that you are called McIntyre and your husband is called Carson. If I was you I'd take a bit more care, lest Sheriff Tucker and Cassidy decide to do a bit of checking. They are mighty suspicious people and Tucker misses nothing.' He paused for several seconds, and then he smiled a tired but friendly smile. 'What do you want me to call you, ma'am?'

'Just call me Sal. I'll think of a way of explaining the name when I need to.' She turned and walked towards the door, and then she paused, looked over her shoulder and smiled. 'And thanks, Mr Dawson. Thanks for everything.'

Sal suddenly felt ravenously hungry. She remembered that there was a supper waiting for her and as she entered the house she was almost overcome by the smell of hot food being prepared by Margy.

She poked her head round the door and sniffed appreciatively.

'Ready when you are, Sal!'

'Thanks, Margy. I'll be there in five seconds flat.'

She sat down to a relaxed meal and, for the first time in a long while she felt clean and civilized. Margy had cooked an enormous stew with both bread and dumplings and they ate at a leisurely pace, exchanging stories; Frank and Margy extolling the many virtues of John Miles. After they had eaten their fill, Margy lit two oil lamps and they sat in front of the fire nursing mugs of strong coffee and talked about the current state of Redwood.

'Darned shame,' Frank mused. 'It was a good town. Till Cassidy came.'

'Shep Cassidy!' Margy spat out the name with a venom which shocked Sal. 'He's a murderous wild dog and should be cut down. He's killed some good men. . . .'

'We don't know that for sure, Margy. It's just rumour and hearsay.'

'Shha!' Margy exhaled angrily. 'You know as well as I do that he's as guilty as hell . . . and hell's where he's going to rot!'

Frank and Sal sat in silence, staring at the crackling log fire. Sal was in fact weighing up the situation in which she found herself. She knew that she was able to kill and she knew that there were at least three major adversaries and, she felt pretty certain, at least two others. That made it five trained and ruthless killers. At least. All were apparently devoid of compassion or conscience. Whereas Frank couldn't prove that they were killers, she could. But could she exact revenge, justice or whatever it was she was after?

One woman against five trained gunmen. One woman who'd made at least three bad mistakes but who had been about as lucky as a four leaf clover tied to a rabbit's foot.

# CHAPTER EIGHT

## REUBEN

Reuben Kane raised himself to his feet then almost toppled over as he tried to pull his boots on.

'Why the hell didn't you tell me she'd gone after them? Damn fool woman'll be killed sure as hell!'

John Miles watched him but didn't offer any help.

'I didn't tell you cos I know what you're like and I know you'll be after them. You just weren't well enough.'

Reuben was reaching for his gun belt and he snarled angrily.

'Damn it, Miles! She'll be a calf to the slaughter with those animals.'

Eve Miles stood with her hands on her hips, facing Reuben with a solid determined expression. She reached for a large cast iron pan which hung from the wall.

'Reuben Kane, get back in to bed this instance or, so help me, I'll hit you with this pan till you see all the stars in the heavens! Just wait for a few days and John'll be able to go with you.'

Reuben raised his eyebrows and smiled a slight, nervous smile before speaking in a quiet, measured tone.

'Eve, I'm sorry but I've got to go. I can't lie here knowing where she's gone. There's nowhere to go 'cept Redwood so that's where I'm heading. If she's doubled back then I can't do anything. The trail will be cold so I've got to take the gamble. I'll ride careful, Eve, and the doc will give me some dressings and ointment so I'll be fine.'

She looked at him for a long time. Her eyes were sad but she was resigned and she hung the pan back on the hook.

'I guess if you don't go you'll never forgive yourself. You're a stubborn, stupid man, Reuben, but I can see that you've got to go.'

They watched as Reuben fastened his gun belt and checked his weapons. John Miles went to fetch his friend's horse and as Reuben ate a small meal with Eve, John led the animal to the door. Reuben tipped his hat forward against the sun and nodded at Miles. Miles nodded back. He wondered if his friend had finally taken on more than he could handle and he wondered if he would ever see him alive again.

'Good luck, Reuben. Be careful, old friend.'

'I will, John. I'll see you when we get back.'

'*We?*'

Reuben looked a mite embarrassed, then he grinned.

'We . . . Me 'n' Sal.' Then he was gone.

# CHAPTER NINE

## DEATH OF A SHERIFF

Sal McIntyre lay in her bed looking up at the sloping ceiling. Her mind was whirling and a small voice kept repeating that she was about to commit a catastrophic error. She kept wondering if what she was doing made any sense. Perhaps it would be better to leave things to the law? Then she remembered Frank reminding her that nothing had been proved and she knew deep down that the law would never catch Cassidy and his men.

She needed to work out a strategy. She needed to take the battle to her enemies and somehow load the odds in her favour. In a straight fight she had no hope. Somehow she had to even the balance. Not for a moment did she consider that the odds were hopeless and that she was doomed to failure if she took on Cassidy.

It was a long time before she fell into a disturbed and fitful sleep, assailed by nightmares in which she smelt

Shep Cassidy's hot breath on her face and felt his rough, unshaven face on her cheek. Then she was in a fast flowing river and Ed was being dragged away from her by the current. The Davies Brothers, although clearly dead and displaying the wounds which she had inflicted, were standing in front of her on the surface of the water and laughing as they prevented her from saving him. She tried desperately to get past them but they had immense strength and they blocked her way. She drew her guns and fired at point blank range, blasting them until she had emptied both guns . . . but they were still standing, laughing and shrieking obscenities at her. Then, as Ed finally disappeared from view and she climbed wearily on to the river bank, they walked towards her, two grinning death heads. She was rooted to the spot, paralysed by fear. Then they were on her.

She woke with a start, drenched in sweat and shaking violently, then she got out of bed and peered out of the window. On the steps of the saloon, illuminated by the orange glow of the lights shining through the doorway, a small group of cowboys shared anecdotes and laughed amiably. Sheriff Tucker was talking to a man who sported a smart long black coat and a black hat. The man was swaying slightly and Sal assumed that he was very drunk. He turned and walked away from the sheriff.

Tucker shouted at the man.

'Turn and face me!'

The man in black turned and faced him. Sal guessed that Tucker was going to arrest him, probably for being drunk. Instead, Tucker drew his gun, slowly and deliberately. The man in black stared at the revolver and his eyes widened in fear. He said something to the sheriff which Sal

75

couldn't hear but which, judging by his raised hands, was some sort of plea for mercy. Sheriff Tucker laughed and appeared to share a joke with the man in black, who lowered his hands and grinned in relief. Then Tucker pointed his revolver at the man in what appeared from Sal's distance to be an almost casual manner and he squeezed the trigger. Flame spurted from the barrel and the man pitched backwards, clutching his chest. Tucker walked slowly to where the man lay, twitching in the dust. Once more, the man in black raised his hand to plead with his assassin but it was a fruitless request. Tucker smiled down at him and pumped three more bullets into his head.

Sal's hand flew to her mouth and she emitted a choked, deep throated gurgle. Tucker holstered his gun and walked calmly away, as if he had just exchanged pleas-antries with the man, then he shouted something at the cowboys, ordering them to carry the crumpled body to the building marked *Carpenter, Joiner and Undertaker*. She could see that the cowboys were shocked and scared. One of them, realizing that his shirt was stained with the dead man's blood, vomited in the street.

Sal shut her curtains. It was several hours before she fell briefly into another horror filled doze. This time she dreamt that she was being chased by Sheriff Tucker. She tired of running and turned to face him. As he grinned confidently, she emptied her Winchester into him, watch-ing him die and feeling elated and joyful as he crumpled to the dusty floor.

Sal woke late the following morning. The sun was streaming through the curtains and she washed and dressed, half believing, or at least hoping that the noctur-nal happenings on the street had been part of her nightmare. Indeed, when she looked out onto the street there was no sign of the drama of the previous night. Mr Dawson was brushing dust from the sidewalk outside his shop and the young cowboys who had witnessed the event were riding slowly out of town, probably hoping that they would never return to Redwood.

She seriously wondered if the killing had really happened outside the confines of her own imagination.

Sal was subdued over breakfast and as she absently prodded a slice of bacon, Margy sipped a coffee and looked at her over the rim of the cup.

'Penny fer 'em?'

'Huh?'

'Your thoughts. Penny fer 'em. You were miles away.'

Sal related what she thought she had witnessed the night before, occasionally having to stop as her lips trembled. Margy sat in silence, listening intently and it was only when Sal had finished talking that she spoke.

'Sheriff? Tucker ain't no sheriff. Not in the way that you'd think anyhow. He's just a killer wearing a star which Cassidy gave him after he hired him to do his dirty work. Do you know who the man was that he killed?'

'Never seen him afore. Just a man dressed in black.'

Margy looked thoughtful. 'He wouldn't have been wearing a long black coat, would he? Tall 'n' thin with a foreign lookin' black hat?'

'That's the man.'

Margy shook her head sadly. Her mouth twitched slightly.

'Jack Farrow. A good man. Owns ... *owned* ... the Crossed Snake ranch just out of town. Wife died about a year ago and since then he comes into town and gets drunk about once a week. Shep Cassidy wanted to buy the Crossed Snake but Farrow wouldn't sell. He said the offer was about half of what it's worth. Cassidy said he'd have the ranch one day and told Farrow he'd made a big mistake in not selling. Farrow upset him by saying things about him in the saloon when the whiskey had loosened his tongue. Guess he should've gone when he could. Poor Jack. Nice man. Honest, too.'

She looked grimly at Sal and was about to say something else when there came a tap at the door. Sal heard voices in the hallway.

Margy brushed some crumbs from her clothes, straightened her hair and went to answer the door. She found Sheriff John Tucker standing there, leaning against the veranda support post and chewing on a cheroot. He glanced at Margy and nodded, smiling politely.

'Mornin', Margy. How're you?'

'Fine, Sheriff.' Margy's voice was icy cold and she didn't return the smile. 'What brings you here?'

'Just looking up our visitor. Coupla questions I need to ask her.'

'She's not feeling too good this morning, Sheriff. Seems that something happened in the night which disturbed her sleep. She ain't well enough to receive visitors. What were the questions? Perhaps I can ask her,' she said artfully.

For a split second, Tucker looked nonplussed, then he smiled another broad, cold smile.

'Sorry, Margy. I'd like to be able to tell you. I really would like to tell you but I can't. Official sheriff's business. Kinda confidential. So if you'd kindly ask her to come down. . . .'

'I'm sorry, Sheriff Tucker, but she really ain't in a fit state to be seeing anyone. Perhaps . . .'

Tucker was trying to disguise his anger and there was nothing he would have liked more than to give this woman a good slapping but there were too many people around and even in Redwood, strong men didn't beat up on old ladies unless it was necessary.

He leaned forward and spoke in a mock conspiratorial whisper.

'Just tell her to be at my office at eleven sharp.' He stared at Margy and although his mouth was still upturned in a smile, his eyes were cold and dead. 'An' tell her that if she's late I'll come lookin' fer her.' The threat in the statement was unmistakable but Margy, shaking inside, appeared calm and polite.

'I'll be sure to tell her, Sheriff.'

Tucker nodded, moved his hat back an inch or so, tipped it politely then turned on his heel and left. As he walked through the door he shouted over his shoulder, 'Bye, Margy. And thank you kindly for your cooperation. And don't you go forgetting to tell her.'

Margy leaned against the door and realized that her hands were shaking.

Sal had been standing behind the kitchen door listening to every word. When she emerged Margy stared hard and long at her.

'Sal. What are you *really* here for? You sure as hell seem to be making some powerful enemies.'

Sal stood defiantly for a moment and was going to tell Margy that it was none of her business but even she realized how mean minded that would be and she thought – no, *knew* – that she could trust this woman. She rubbed her mouth and looked at the floor and when her eyes finally met Margy's, she had made her decision.

'I guess I owe it to you to be honest, Margy, as I seem to have involved you in this business, like it or no.'

She looked at the floor again then Margy asked her to sit down. Starting from the murder of her husband Ed, Sal related her story in brutal, honest detail, ending with the murder of Jack Farrow by Sheriff Tucker the previous night. When she finished, both women had tears running down their cheeks and Margy embraced Sal and stroked her hair.

'You poor, poor child. What have those sons of bitches done to you?'

Sal wept convulsively and copiously. She wept for Ed, for herself and for life. It was a full half hour before she finally subsided, laying her head on the table, totally exhausted.

Margy helped her over to the rocking chair and covered her in a blanket and Sal slept a deep sleep, for once untroubled by nightmares. Margy sat and watched the vulnerable looking young woman and four hours later, when Sal opened her eyes, she was still there.

Sal blinked and for a moment she didn't know where she was. Then she saw Margy's smiling face.

'How long . . . what time is it?'

As she spoke a knock came on the front door. She looked at the clock on the mantelpiece. It was eleven thirty. Margy had forgotten to wake her in time for her appointment with Tucker. Sal put her fingers to her lips, asking Margy for silence, then she noiselessly fled to her room, leaving Margy to open the door to Sheriff Tucker.

'Hi, Margy. I jest came to enquire as to what happened

80

to Mrs McIntyre. I got kinda tired waiting. In fact, I got real tired and jest a bit annoyed. Where the hell is she?'

Margy was about to shrug in a non-committal reply when Sal's voice echoed from the parlour.

'I'm in here, Sheriff.'

Tucker went into the parlour and found Sal sitting with her elbows resting on the table. She looked up at him, giving him the benefit of a charming, pretty smile which, for reasons which he didn't fully comprehend, infuriated him.

'Good morning Mrs Cars – or is it McIntyre?'

Sal said nothing, but she continued to fix him with the same dazzling smile. His anger gave way to a feeling of slight confusion. The fact that a pretty young woman seemed to be getting the better of him was rousing his temper. He breathed deeply, determining to remain cool, at least on the surface.

'Now why would you like to be called by two different names, ma'am? Seems kinda strange, wouldn't you say? Kinda like you might have something to hide.' He emphasized his point with an expression created to display a theatrical, over the top confusion. Sal, on the other hand, said nothing and still smiled beatifically. Tucker was growing dangerously angry.

'Y'know what I think, ma'am? Well, I'll tell you what I think. I think your husband was Ed McIntyre, whose murder is described loud and clear on this here poster.' He waved the official poster under her nose.

WANTED!!
Shep Cassidy and Pete Robinson
for the murder of Ed McIntyre. Reward $100

'It came this morning, Mrs McIntyre, and I kinda put two and two together and made four. I knew who you *said* you were but I also knew that our friendly storeowner had sold you stuff. I asked Mrs Evans about the new woman in town and she said, "Oh! That'll be that nice Mrs McIntyre".'

Sal was still sitting impassively, still smiling at him and showing no apparent concern. Tucker moved his face close to hers. She smelled the tobacco and stale alcohol on his breath. He snarled. A deep, guttural snarl.

'By my reckoning, you, ma'am, are a woman tryin' to do a man's work. You are trying to get revenge for your husband. You are after Shep Cassidy and let me tell you, you stupid bitch, that you stand no chance.'

He laughed in her face, then continued, his voice a hissing, hateful sound.

'If – and it's a big if – you are right about who killed your husband, you still stand as much chance as a snowflake in the fires of hell of getting them who killed him. Even if you wuz a gunman you'd have no chance.' His nose was almost touching hers now and he spoke in the same grating whisper. 'You are out of yor depth, little lady. Truly out of yor depth.'

Sal wasn't sure what would happen next. She expected him to make threats, to tell her what would happen to her if she didn't get out of town and forget her business with Shep Cassidy. What he actually did do shocked her. He drew his revolver and held it with the barrel pointing at and almost touching her forehead.

'And now I'm gonna wipe that stoopid smile off your face. Permanently. Sorry, Mrs McIntyre. Nothing personal.' He smiled a broad smile and clicked the hammer back.

The explosion caused by a gun firing in a small room is deafening. It was the last sound that Tucker heard before the agonizing pain in his stomach drove all thought from his mind. He stared at the Winchester rifle which Sally McIntyre had been holding under the table and which had appeared silent and unnoticed. Tucker was flung back from the table and he smashed against the wall. For a moment which seemed like an age he stood there, clutching at the spreading scarlet stain and groaning in agony. Then, in a bizarre parody of Jack Farrow, his hand raised in a plea for mercy.

Sal shook her head very slowly and spoke in a slow imitation of Tucker's own voice.'Maybe you gave a little bit too much notice of your intention, Sheriff Tucker. You know what I think? I think you were outa yor depth. Truly out of yor depth, you murderin' heap of dung. Bit like Jack Farrow, huh? Mebbe a bit like Ed? Waddya think, Sheriff? Do you think you're out of yor depth?'

Tucker's mouth opened and closed like a landed fish. Although no words came he was clearly pleading for his life.

'You may live or die here, Tucker. I'm not a doctor so I couldn't say. But if you live, it'll only be long enough fer the hangman's noose. Believe me, I'd like to finish you off here and now, but I guess that'd make me as bad as you.'

Tucker tried to take a step towards her, arms outstretched as if his intention was to strangle her, then, as if by magic, a Derringer pistol appeared via a sprung holster in his sleeve.

Too late.

Sal fired at point blank range. He was flung backwards again and he was already dead as he hit the wall. With the look of amazement still fixed on his face he slid slowly to the floor.

Margy ran into the room and stared open mouthed at the horror before her. Her home was a scene of devastation. The large figure of Tucker sat in a pose which reminded her of the wooden string puppet which had been her favourite toy when she was a little girl. The flowery wallpaper was covered in splatters of blood and some china ornaments which had adorned the mantelpiece were scattered in pieces around the bulky body of the sheriff. Sal McIntyre was standing in the middle of the room holding a Winchester rifle in her right hand and staring at her victim. Her lips were moving slightly as if she was talking quietly to herself and Margy knew that the young woman was not even aware of her presence in the room.

Slowly, very slowly, Margy's hand went to her mouth and she covered her lips before breaking down with a wail. She turned her attention to the body again and saw a red stain beginning to seep into the light rag rug which she had made some thirty years ago. Her home, a place of quiet and refuge for so many years – the place where she had brought up her family and seen births, baptisms, illnesses, weddings and funerals had in a matter of seconds become a place of violence and death. She knew she would never erase the scene from her mind and she sat on the floor and wept.

The sound brought Sal out of her private world and she stared at the scene of carnage. Margy sat, distraught and Sal wanted to comfort her and tell her everything was going to be OK but instead she heard her own voice, speaking as if it wasn't engaged to her brain.

'Hi, Margy. Glad I've got a witness. Not every day you get to kill a sheriff. Even a murdering liar like Sheriff Tucker.'

Without any display of emotion she checked her sidearms. She felt pretty certain that Tucker would have spoken to Cassidy before meeting with her. If that was the case then Cassidy would be aware that she wasn't a casual visitor. Amazingly, no one had come to see what the gunfire was about. Then again, gunfire wasn't unusual with the drunken men in the street and she reasoned that Cassidy wouldn't be unduly perturbed by gunfire coming from Margy and Frank's house. Indeed, he would have been expecting gunfire, assuming that Tucker had dispatched her, rather than the opposite.

She took another look at Margy, who was still staring at the body and shaking. The horror of what had happened slowly dawned on her and she emerged from her shocked trance.

'I ... I'm sorry, Margy. It was him or me. I had no choice.'

It seemed to Sal to be a wholly inadequate explanation to a friend whose life she had just turned upside down, but Margy nodded dumbly, then averted her eyes from the body and nodded at Sal.

'Time for you to get out before Cassidy finds out what's happened, Sal.'

Without another word, Sal gave Margy a faint smile of gratitude, then turned and walked out into the street. She tried to walk slowly, to avoid drawing attention to herself. Her insides were shaking and her mind was beginning to whirl. What was she becoming? She had just killed a man, albeit a violent killer. But she was feeling no remorse. How could anyone kill – take the life of another person – and feel nothing?

When she mounted her horse she wanted to kick in her heels and hightail out of Redwood forever. Instead, she nudged the horse's flank and rode at an even pace up the main street, expecting with every step to hear Shep Cassidy's voice ordering her to stop, or to feel the sharp pain of a bullet ripping into her back. But there was nothing except the muffled sound of horse hoofs on the sandy ground and the heat of the sun on her back.

She had arrived in Redwood as the hunter. Now, she reflected, she was the quarry.

# CHAPTER TEN

## COULSON

Reuben Kane had ridden hard trailing Sal McIntyre. It had been pretty easy to follow her. Basically he kept his ears open and followed the body count, knowing that she was trailing Cassidy's men with revenge on her mind. He was glad to reach Redwood and he wearily dismounted before tying his horse to the rail. He was standing outside the saloon and his intention was to rid himself of the cloying dust in his throat by sinking a beer, but first he surveyed the street. People were going about their everyday business and Mr Dawson was making neat stacks of sacks of flour outside the emporium. The livery stable boy was leading a sleek black stallion into the stable, which meant that someone else had just arrived in town. A middle-aged woman was walking hand in hand with a little girl.

Suddenly there was a shot from somewhere down the street. Reuben's right hand instinctively went for his gun and rested on the butt, ready for action. He was the only one to show any concern. A few seconds elapsed and there was another shot. The residents of Redwood still appeared unmoved and continued with their routines as if the shots had never been fired.

In truth, as Sal had already discovered, a couple of shots seemed as commonplace here as a horse passing down the main street. Reuben relaxed then walked thoughtfully into the saloon and ordered a beer.

'Comin' right up, sir. That all?'

'For the moment.'

Reuben leaned on the bar and looked at the reflection in the big mirror. He drained the glass in one long draught, washing the dust of the ride from his throat, then he smiled at the barman.

'Tell me something. Has there been a lone woman riding into town this last day or so? 'Bout thirty or so. Slim, tall an' black hair.'

The barman looked warily at him. Redwood wasn't the sort of town where you gave information about people without checking who was asking and why. He deliberately avoided eye contact and stared with studied concentration at the glass in his hand as he answered.

'Who wants to know?'

'Oh, just an old friend. I've got some news for her from back home.'

The barman continued to examine the glass which he was now polishing as if his life depended on it and he thought for a couple of seconds before answering.

'Can't say I've noticed anyone like that,' he lied. A lone woman arriving in Redwood was news. He was fully aware of Sal's arrival but he considered, for reasons of self-preservation, that it was none of his business.

Reuben had picked up on the slight hesitation and the

reluctance to make eye contact and he knew that the man was prevaricating.

Sal *was* in Redwood. He was certain of it. It was a pensive Reuben Kane who walked through the saloon doors out into the heat and the brilliant brightness of the street.

Reuben's routine – and it was one which had been responsible for saving his life on more than one occasion – was to sit on the sidewalk and survey any new town in which he found himself. He found a rickety old chair and sat in his familiar pose, hat low over his eyes, watching what was happening, working out what were the most likely places for someone to hide in the event of a gun-fight. He gauged the angle of the light to ensure that if the worst happened he wouldn't be faced with the sun shining in his eyes and blinding him.

Over the street he could see the livery stable boy had finished settling the black stallion in. The kid was sitting in the shade on a barrel outside the stables, chewing on a piece of straw and drawing lines in the dust with a stick.

Reuben rose slowly from the chair, unhitched his horse from the rail and led it slowly across the street to the livery stable, where he handed the reins to the boy, before telling him to water and feed the horse. He looked at the sleek black stallion, as if he hadn't seen it before. He knew that anyone who could afford such a steed was comfortably off, if not downright rich. Placed on the wooden rail next to the horse was a beautifully crafted saddle which bore the inscription *A. Coulson*. He called the boy over.

'Say, this here stallion looks like the horse of a friend of mine. I didn't realize he was headed in the same direction as me. Can you tell me where he's gone?'

'You say he's a friend?' asked the boy warily. 'How do I know that yor telling the truth, mister?'

Reuben scratched his head, as if deep in thought.

'I guess you don't, son.' Then he smiled as if he had had a brainwave. 'Tell you what. I'll describe my friend to you, then you'll know I'm on the level. You can even ask me questions about him.'

The boy smiled a half trusting smile.

'OK, mister.' He sounded unsure and cautious. 'What's this friend of yors like?'

'Well, he likes steak and eggs and dark haired women.'

The boy laughed and relaxed a tad.

'Naw. When I said what's he *like* I meant what does he *look* like, not what he likes to eat and . . . well, y'know . . .'

'Oh, I see. Well, he's slim, tall – about six foot and more – usually wears a grey frock coat and a sort of sissy frilly shirt. Most of the women say he's a good looker too.'

The boy smiled.

'That's yor man, mister. He's gone to the restaurant. Lee Hing's – you cain't miss it. He wuz going to meet Shep Cassidy.' The boy stopped suddenly, wondering if he'd given too much information. Reuben grinned disarmingly and tossed the boy a coin.

'Thanks, sonny. He'll be mighty pleased to see me. You see, it's a kind of surprise. Can you keep a secret?'

'Sure can.'

'Well, I'm his cousin and it's his birthday tomorrow so I'm expecting his sister to arrive any time and we've got a kinda secret celebration arranged for him. That's why I need to be able to trust you not to tell a soul.'

Reuben bit his tongue at his stupid mistake. The boy didn't seem to have noticed the holes in Reuben's story.

Reuben wondered if he would suddenly realize later that he had said he didn't know Abe Coulson was around and then had later said he had a surprise celebration planned. He scrutinized the boy's expression but it conveyed no sign of confusion or mistrust. He nodded at the boy. 'I appreciate that, son. Remember. Not a word.'

He tossed another coin in the direction of the boy, who caught it deftly and smiled a broad smile, indicating that the deal had been struck.

'You can rely on me, mister. Wild horses wouldn't drag it from me.'

'Thanks, son. I appreciate that.'

Reuben sauntered back to the chair outside the saloon. He glanced up and down the street but there was no sign of Cassidy or any of his men. His brow was furrowed in thought. He was sure now of what he had guessed when he had first seen the stallion. It was owned by Abe Coulson.

Coulson was an easy man to spot on account of the fact that he always wore the same style of immaculate light grey frock coat and fancy silk shirts. He was also strikingly handsome and charming but even way back in his twenties he had earned a reputation for being a hard, ruthless killer who could be hired by anyone, whichever side of the law they were on, for the right amount of money. Reuben cast around in his memory and recalled his previous meeting with Abe Coulson.

He had been on business in a small backwoods town called Holme when Coulson had arrived. Coulson had been aware that a small time gunman called Walt Smith was looking for him. He had killed Smith's nephew in a gunfight and Walt Smith was seeking revenge.

Smith had spotted Coulson getting off his horse in the

main street and immediately drawn his Remington and aimed at Coulson's back with the intention of giving him no chance. Reuben had expected him to fire but instead, Walt Smith made his fatal mistake.

'Coulson!' The shout had echoed down the street. 'Coulson, you murdering son of a bitch! Prepare to mee—'

The sentence was never completed. With amazing speed and grace, Coulson had spun on the balls of his feet and flung himself sideways, simultaneously drawing his gun with his left hand. Before Smith had time to squeeze the trigger on his Remington, Coulson's Colt had fired twice and two deep red patches had appeared on Smith's shirt, signifying where the bullets had entered before piercing his heart.

Coulson, Reuben noted, was not only ruthless, he was fast and accurate.

There was a lot for Reuben Kane to ponder as he sat in the shade outside the saloon in Redwood. He leaned back in the chair and watched the townsfolk go about their business. As he squinted under the brim he saw a woman riding a horse up the street. She was riding slowly.

There was something familiar about her.

Reuben's mouth curled upwards in a smile of recognition. It was Sal McIntyre.

# CHAPTER ELEVEN

## RIDING OUT

Sal McIntyre walked slowly to the livery stables and asked the boy to prepare her horse. She needed to get out of town and into the hills where she would have some space to empty her mind. She shuddered as the boy handed over the reins, then she swung herself into the saddle. The words of Reuben Kane and John Miles kept repeating in her head and she realized that they had been right. She had killed men, almost without compunction or regret. She knew deep down that she had changed as a person and the realization disturbed her. She wondered if she would ever be able to return to what most people would call a normal life, or if the changes in her were permanent. Deep down in her gut she knew that she still had to deal with Shep Cassidy, Crazy Pete Robinson and in all probability Abraham Coulson. She felt on the one hand that she had no choice in the matter and that she could never go on living until Ed was avenged but part of her was drowning in doubt and guilt. Her determination to avenge Ed's murder had been the direct cause of the deaths of several people. She had killed people in cold blood and she couldn't, even to herself, pretend that she had simply had justice in her mind when she had killed the Davies boys. She had been driven by a mixture of motives, one of which was pure hate. She had felt satisfaction – no, not satisfaction – almost elation, mixed with a terrible guilt when she killed them.

'But they were vermin, Sal.' She suddenly realized that she was talking out loud to herself again. Vermin or not, she had experienced strange emotions when taking human lives. It wasn't something she cared to dwell on and she seriously wondered if she had sunk to the level of Shep Cassidy and his ilk, who killed for fun.

Such were her thoughts as she rode up the main street towards the edge of town.

The days with Reuben Kane had taught her a lot and as she rode she scanned the street from side to side to ensure that there was no sign of anyone who might be a danger to her. Her left hand held the reins loosely, within distance of her Colt. Her right hand was left free, resting inches above the Winchester in its holster on the side of her mount. She reckoned that the saloon would be a possible place for an enemy to fire at her through the swing doors out of the darkness beyond. Glancing to her right, she saw a familiar figure sitting on a rickety chair next to the saloon door, his hat pulled down covering his eyes and his limp looking hand lying on the butt of his sidearm. She turned her horse toward the saloon and dismounted in front of him. She was smiling and she was about to wake him when he spoke from under the hat.

'Hello, Sal,' he drawled. 'Try to look as if you ain't recognized me.' Sal didn't realize that he had seen her and
was surprised when she heard the voice. Anyone not in
earshot wouldn't have known he had even spoken.
Indeed, they would have noticed nothing as neither Sal
nor Reuben showed any sign of recognition.

The marshal continued in his quiet drawl.

'Good to see you. Pretend you ain't seen me and look
like you are checking your saddle or something. Take your
time doing it, so it don't look suspicious, then look like
you've sorted whatever problem you had and get on your
horse and ride north. Follow the trail past Jack Farrow's
place – that's the Crossed Snake ranch. There's a rocky
outcrop about a mile on and an old cabin next to it. I'll
follow you after I've left a bit of time. I want to ensure that
if anyone's looking, they won't realize that we're con-
nected. I'll meet you there at the cabin. There's lots we
need to talk about if you're still intent on your damn fool
plan to get Cassidy. I'd like you to consider a few points
afore you get us both killed.'

Sal was annoyed that he'd referred to her plan in such
a derogatory way. She wanted to round on him and to
point out to him that she'd never asked him to come to
Redwood and he could get the hell back to wherever he
came from. But she knew that to show any sign of recognition could be a fatal mistake so she held her tongue and
went through the motions of tightening her saddle, then
led her pony back into the street before mounting and
riding north out of town. When her annoyance had subsided she was surprised, as she rode away, to realize just
how pleased she was to have met up with Reuben and
indeed she found it hard not to look back. Naturally she

was relieved to know that she had an ally against Cassidy and his partners. But there was more than that. She was . . . well, she was genuinely happy to see him. She had, she told herself, felt alone and vulnerable and now she would have Reuben to talk to as a friend.

'But you'll have a piece of my mind first, Reuben Kane.' She became aware that she had spoken her thoughts out loud yet again and laughed quietly to herself. 'This talkin' to yerself is becoming a habit, Sal.'

The dry, dusty road led out of town and she turned the brim of her hat down to shield her eyes against the blazing sun which scorched her from a blue, cloudless sky. She pulled her neckerchief up around her mouth in an ineffective attempt to keep out the dust. She passed the Crossed Snake and before her lay a wilderness, dry and arid. Years ago a crazy prospector had arrived, believing for no discernible reason that there was gold in the ground. His crazy scheme had come to nothing and he had left penniless, leaving the hut which she saw in the distance as the only evidence that he had existed at all. When she reached the hut she sat outside, leaning against the wall under a dilapidated wooden canopy which provided the only shade from the relentless sun. She had a view of the road which she had just travelled and she sat in the enormous silence, letting her mind drift but simultaneously keeping a close eye on her surroundings. A lizard scuttled across a small rock at her feet then stopped and looked at her in surprise before disappearing into a hole, its tail flicking at her as it went to earth.An hour passed without any sign of Reuben Kane and she began to wonder if she was at the correct venue. Perhaps there was another rocky outcrop and old hut?

Unlikely. She shielded her eyes from the sun and peered to the horizon. Then she saw him. He was quite close but had somehow stayed out of view, keeping to the small dry river beds which criss-crossed behind the hills. He obviously didn't want to be seen. Eventually he reached the slope which led up to the cabin and she heard the muffled sound of hoofs made by his pony and saw the dust cloud which swirled lazily around the rider.

When he reached her she didn't stand up and he didn't dismount. He smiled and nodded. She reciprocated and there was silence for a few seconds as if they were both embarrassed and tongue tied.

'Hi, Sal. You OK?'

'I guess. And you? Are you recovered?'

He nodded, smiled and dismounted and she slowly rose to face him.

'I was worried about you, Sal. Wondered what had happened. What you—'

'I was worried too, Reuben,' she interrupted. 'About you. I'm sorry about what ha—'

'No need. It happened. No sense in raking over it. Can't change the past and regrets are energy wasted.'

They stood facing each other in a slightly confused, slightly uncomfortable silence. Neither knew what to say. Reuben broke the silence.

'I ain't seen Cassidy or Coulson. It stands to reason that they ain't seen me or I'd probably be taking the long sleep somewheres. I can't be sure but I don't think people are generally good at keeping secrets from the likes of Cassidy so my guess is that they know I'm around by now.'

'Would they recognize us if'n they saw us, Reuben?'

'Me? Definitely. You? I'm not sure. They only saw you in

the heat of battle when—'

'Not quite.' Sal's voice was flat. 'Shep Cassidy and Pete Robinson saw me before the shootout. After they murdered my hu—'

Reuben clasped both hands to his face.

'Sal. I'm sorry. It was stupid of me. I'd forgotten about the . . . the. . . .' His voice faded away and he stood before her like an embarrassed schoolboy. Sal simply smiled very gently and spoke in an over firm voice.

'No point in regrets, Reuben. The past is gone. So if we are to stand a chance we must see *them* before they see *us*.'

'That's about it. You can be sure if they see us they'll come out shooting.' He nodded, still feeling embarrassed after his comments. Then he took some provisions from his saddle bags and for the next few minutes he avoided either conversation or eye contact by concentrating on making a fire, after which he brewed some coffee. When he turned back, Sal was sitting on a bench, fashioned from some logs and an old plank, staring quietly at the darkening sky as dusk began to steal the brightness from the sun. She looked beautiful, pensive and melancholy as she stared into space. Reuben stood watching her in silence for some time. 'Coffee?' He broke the spell with his request and she jumped slightly, as if she had not been aware of his presence, then she nodded and he poured her a mug.

'You looked deep in thought. I'm sorry, Sal. I guess I raked up memories.'

She looked down and ran her fingers round the rim of the mug and he saw that she was near to tears. For a full five minutes they sat in silence, sipping the strong, black liquid.

'I think I would like to.'

'Huh? Like to what?'

'Talk about it. I seem to have bin holding everything in forever and I'm afraid that one day I'll just burst.'

Reuben didn't press her and he remained silent, waiting for her to continue.

'It all happened so fast.' Her gaze and voice were wistful and she continued speaking in a more distant, emotionless tone. She was still afraid that if she really started to cry she might never stop, but her apparently calm demeanour was betrayed by a slight tremor in her voice.

'I was a rancher's wife. A contented wife. Loving and loved. I'd never killed anyone. Never even crossed my mind that I *would* kill anyone. Now . . . now I've gunned men down and I've killed them without regret or remorse. More than that . . . I felt *satisfied* when I killed 'em. Deeply, profoundly satisfied. Yet the Bible tells me I shouldn't kill. The Bible says that vengeance is the Lord's. Well, I sure as hell was satisfied when I avenged Ed. I guess I can explain that to myself but the real trouble is that part of me actually *enjoyed* it.'

She remembered the deaths of Johnny and Rab Davies. She felt confused, guilty and weary.

'I can't even say I didn't know what I was doing. I knew that what I was doing was bad. A voice told me to stop. My conscience, I guess. But I taunted Rab Davies afore I killed him. I knew that I was going to kill him but I actually taunted him.'

She turned towards Reuben, her face, still slightly bruised, features shining orange in the glow from the fire.

'Does that make me a bad person, Reuben?'

Reuben flicked the last drops of his coffee into the fire, making it sizzle.

'I don't rightly know about what a preacher might say, Sal, but to my mind it just makes you human like the rest of us. Those men had taken what you loved the most and you were hurtin' bad . . . you still are hurtin' bad. When we're hurt and confused we tend to behave in ways that we can't explain. We do things we'd never normally do.

'But when it's done, we can't change anything by regretting it. I guess that what's important is that we've just got to learn and move on. Mebbe as a better person. Mebbe not. But the fact that you're regretting it now means that you can and will change if you can start to forgive yourself. It's only the future that counts now, Sal. The past is something we can't change. Move on from it and forgive yourself.'

Reuben Kane rarely spoke more than a few words at a time and he had surprised even himself. Now, as he stood staring at Sal's profile, he spoke again.

'What are you thinking of now?'

'Ed. My husband.' Her voice was still distant and had a dreamlike quality.

'D'you think about him a lot?'

'What do you think? He was my husband, damn it!' she retorted sharply. Then she muttered an apology. 'Sorry. Yes, I think about Ed. Almost all the time. I loved him more than anyone or anything I ever knew. I guess I still do. Mebbe I always will.'

Tears were streaming down her cheeks. She wept silently and he wanted to hold her to him but instead he stood back in silence. He ached inside seeing her in pain, knowing that he could do nothing to assuage it. And so they remained, in a silence that was both distant and intimate. The world was silent except for the occasional snorting of their horses and the crackle of the fire.

The enormous sky above them looked down, impassive, eternal and mysterious.

Some time later, they sat underneath the stars talking. Sal had focussed her mind on the present and was asking Reuben questions about the best way to deal with Cassidy and his friends. She was resolutely determined to go into Redwood and finish Cassidy and his mob but she still hadn't worked out any strategy for doing so and seemed intent on walking into Redwood with guns blazing.

Reuben was more pragmatic and he talked firmly and rationally. He was still trying to weigh up the odds in his own mind and to find a way in which he and Sal would have some chance, however slight, of achieving her objective and surviving. His preferred method was to bide his time and pick them off one by one, even if it took years. Sal wouldn't even countenance such a plan.

'I want to settle it now so's that I can get on with my life. Every moment that passes with Cassidy and Robinson unpunished is a moment longer afore I can get back to living. I'd rather die than go on living knowing that . . .' Her voice faded and angry tears took over. Reuben took his chance to try and inject some realism into their plan of action.

'. . . So it looks like we have Cassidy, Crazy Pete and Abe Coulson to contend with. Coulson's definitely in town. My guess is that they've got a couple more to help them. They need people to keep order when they're away from town and they'll have the sheriff in their . . .'

'They had a sheriff. Sheriff Tucker. They ain't got one no more. I killed him.'

To Sal's surprise Reuben said nothing. She looked into

his eyes, searching for a reaction but saw none. She didn't know if he had already been told about Tucker, but whether he had or hadn't he gave nothing away. Instead, he continued to guide the conversation back to tactics.

'So that leaves Cassidy, Robinson, Coulson and probably some deputy sheriff.'

'I guess so. So what do we do? Shall we take them?'

Reuben picked up a piece of wood which had broken off from the shed and he drew a pattern in the sand. He was thinking.

'I think mebbe I should go back to town and find out if there is a deputy, who he is and how fast he is with a gun. Then we'll know what we are up against an' we can work out what to do. Looks like it'll be four agin two at best. I'd wager they'll have at least a couple of hired killers, which'll make six. Coulson is probably the fastest of them all.'

'I know.' Sal's voice was matter of fact and for a moment Reuben wondered why, then he remembered her telling him about Coulson outdrawing her at a competition.

Even after listening to Sal's invective, Reuben was desperately trying to think of an argument that would persuade her to give up on her suicide mission. The two of them stood no chance, unless perhaps they could split Cassidy's forces and have the element of surprise.

'I think it's best if you don't go into town tonight, Sal.' He looked at her to gauge her reaction and he was encouraged when she didn't respond negatively. Cautiously, he proceeded to outline his half worked out plan.

'Cassidy will be pretty wild about Tucker. He'll be looking fer blood – your blood. We'll need a good plan to make sure he doesn't get it. I brung some food supplies in

102

my saddle bags and mebbe you could stay here in the hut tonight. If we both go to town we'll be spotted. It's not often a woman comes riding alone into a town like Redwood and you'd stand out like a pig in a bathtub. If I go back to town alone I might be able to get around without being seen. I can see Frank and Margy and ask around about the deputy an' such. I'll come back at dawn. I cain't see anyone travelling this road tonight, but best tether your pony behind the rocks and outta sight.'

It made sense. Neither wanted to leave the other but it was without doubt the safest course to take. Reuben saddled his pony, then as he straightened up Sal put her hands on his shoulders, reached up on tiptoes and kissed him lightly on the cheek.

'Be careful, Reuben. Cassidy and his scum will recognize you.' Then, as if to cover herself she added, 'I sure as hell don't want to have to take them on by myself.'

Reuben smiled and tipped his hat back.

'I ain't aiming to meet up with them, Sal.' He climbed up on to his horse and looked down at her. 'Don't worry. Any sign of trouble and I'll hightail it back to here. See you later.'

Reuben's lazy smile didn't reflect what he was feeling. Questions tumbled around in his head. What if Cassidy had heard that he was in town? He knew that if this was the case he was a dead man. Cassidy and his bunch would be prepared and waiting to gun him down on sight. He had tossed up the odds in his mind and decided it was worth the risk to delay Sal's visit to Redwood. This way, if she still insisted on going on her mission of vengeance, he knew that he would be at her side. They had come too far together for him to desert her now. Not only that, he was

103

beginning to have stronger feelings for Sal than he admitted even to himself. He knew they could never be reciprocated. She still loved Ed and hopefully, when this was all over, she'd return to her ranch, start over and probably, in the distant future, find someone else. His growing affection for her was making him feel vulnerable. He knew that when he was fighting alone he could work out the odds in a cool, dispassionate manner to ensure that they were in his favour. If Sal was around . . . well, he wasn't sure exactly what was going on in his mind but he knew that he wouldn't be able to concentrate on the job with his usual single minded, ruthless coolness if he was worrying about her.

So he vowed to find out exactly who they were up against. He needed to know numbers, what they looked like and just how good they were.

As he entered the main street he slowed his horse almost to a standstill and he searched again for any vantage points where one of Cassidy's men could be hiding. There were too many to cover so he rode down the middle of the street until he arrived at the house belonging to Frank and Margy.

He knocked lightly on the door and Margy appeared. She looked grey and worried and glanced nervously over Reuben's shoulder before ushering him into the house.

She sat at the big table and related what had happened since Sal's departure. She had had Deputy Sheriff Tom James with her for most of the day questioning her about Sheriff Tucker's death. Margy had explained to them that Sal McIntyre was just a paying guest, no more and no less. She had never seen the woman before and the likelihood was that she would never set eyes on her again. As soon as she closed the door behind the deputy, the undertaker had called and removed the body, leaving the blood stained floor and wall for her to clean as best she could. It was a gruesome, gruelling task. Her hands were shaking and Reuben could see that she was near to breaking point. Frank appeared from the garden, where he had been burning the carpet and he started fussing round his wife like a mother hen, looking worried, shocked and confused.

Reuben owed them an explanation even though Sal had told Margy what had led up to the killing but when he tried to speak she waved his faltering words aside.

'No need to explain, Mr Kane. It's done. I guess I understand the whys and wherefores. A man like Tucker was an affront to human decency . . . but it's in my home.' Her voice faded away and Frank held her in his arms, trying to quell her shaking as she sobbed violently.

They sat round the table and talked. Reuben wasn't sure if he should tell them what Sal's plan was but after a while Margy seemed to calm down and he told her what was happening and hoped that Sal was right when she had told him that the couple could be trusted.

'So if anyone asks, just stick with your story – which is true – that you don't know where she's gone but you guess she's hightailed it after murdering Tucker.'

The old couple nodded in unison, still clutching each other closely as if they were one person.

Reuben nodded, not knowing what to say.

'Can you tell me anything about the deputy sheriff, Frank?'

Frank pressed some tobacco into the bowl of an ancient pipe before standing up.

105

'Come outside into the garden, Reuben. I never smoke in the house. Margy cain't abide the smell of tobacco.' He nodded towards the door and Reuben followed him out into the small garden which fronted on to the street. The remains of the carpet were smouldering, giving off an acrid smoke. Frank lit his pipe, tapping the burning tobacco embers before nodding in the direction of the sheriff's office.

'You see the sheriff's office over the street?'

'I see it.'

'Well, the feller sitting on a barrel whittlin' is Deputy Sheriff Tom James. He'll be in charge now that Tucker's dead.'

Reuben pretended to glance along the street but in reality he only had eyes for the deputy sheriff. Tom James was a big, bulky man with a thick, black beard. Leaning against the wooden barrel was a Winchester rifle and tucked into his belt, unholstered, were two hand guns, the makes of which Reuben couldn't identify from this distance.

'What can you tell me about him, Frank?'

Frank blew a small cloud of tobacco smoke and a rich aroma of good quality tobacco drifted past Reuben.

'He's a Cassidy man through and through. Too stupid to do anything off his own bat but totally loyal to Cassidy. The Winchester's his weapon of choice and I've never heard of him using his sidearms so I suspect he ain't fast or accurate – but I could be wrong. He's strong as a bull and beats up on people jest fer the hell of it. He's killed a few in his time but as far as I'm aware never in a fair fight. Him 'n' Tucker were the perfect pair. Sadistic, no compunction and totally immoral.'

106

'They sound like ideal companions for Shep Cassidy.'

'Too true.'

'Thanks, Frank. And are there any others apart from Cassidy, Robinson and Coulson that I ought to know about?'

'Not as far as I'm aware, Reuben. But they're pretty formidable. Ruthless. Not an ounce of decency between the whole damn bunch of them.' He prodded the carpet with his boot, causing a shower of sparks which fell harmlessly to the ground, then he looked at the small vegetable patch, deep in thought.

'Reuben, I know how you feel. I really do. But I don't think that you an' Sal would have much chance against them. In fact, unless something mighty strange happens, I don't think you have any chance at all.'

Reuben shot Frank a sardonic smile.

'Me neither, Frank. Me neither. Snowballs in hell would have more hope. Problem is, Sal's going in, with or without me.'

They stood in silence for a while, watching the smoke curl up from the rug.

'Tell me, Frank, do you know where any of them spend the night?'

Frank tapped his pipe on the fence before answering.

'Robinson will be in the Crazy Lady. He drinks there most nights till he's drunk then chooses himself a saloon girl for the night. Up the stairs. Last room on the left. Number 4. Cassidy and the others'll be at the big house on the right at the end of the street past the Crazy Lady. There'll be two men hanging around. Hell, I'd forgotten all about them. They're Eli Brown and Bill Pierce. Those two stay up all night in the Crazy Lady jest in case someone decides they want to ventilate Cassidy, if you understand my meaning.'

Reuben pricked up his ears. Two more to be dealt with.

'What do you know about Brown and Pierce?'

'Hired killers. Arrived here from nowhere about a year ago. Most of us thought they was on the run from the law. Still do. Anyway, they arrived and Cassidy hired them as bodyguards. Both use Colts as weapons of choice. Both got a name for being accurate and deadly.'

'How will I recognize them?'

'They usually arrive at the sheriff's office about this time every day. If you sit outside, you'll see them.'

Reuben and Frank sat on the bench just down from the sheriff's office, looking for all the world like two friends enjoying a smoke and relaxing. When two men rode up to the office and hitched their horses to the rail, Frank nodded. Reuben watched them, absorbing every detail.

'Taller one's Brown,' Frank whispered.

When he had seen enough, Reuben raised himself slowly from the bench and ambled back to where his horse stood patiently waiting. He mounted and nodded at Frank.

'Unless I can persuade her to see sense we may be here tomorrow.'

'Is there nothing I can say or do to convince you to give it up? If you refuse to come mebbe she'll see how crazy it is and give up on the idea. You 'n' Sal don't—'

'I know. We don't have a chance. You're right, Frank. But I sure as hell don't think Sal will listen and it's even surer that I ain't going to let her come alone.'

The conversation was interrupted by Margy, who appeared in the doorway with a canvas bag.

'Food. You'll need it. Pie, bread and bacon. Now get on with you and get to that woman.' She turned abruptly and went back into the house without waiting for thanks. Reuben didn't have the heart to tell her he'd already got some provisions. And Margy's pie sure smelled good.

Reuben rode slowly out of town, watched by Frank. The old man stood at his doorway, watching the receding horseman until he was almost lost from view. He felt a hand on his shoulder and realized that his wife had joined him.

'Damn it, Margy, if I was thirty years younger I'd be riding in with them tomorrow.'

'I know, Frank. And I'd probably damn well join you to free our town of this scum.'

Reuben finally disappeared from view into the hills. Frank heard Margy's whisper from behind him.

'Good luck, Reuben Kane. And God speed.'

John Dawson was sweeping the sidewalk and he paused and waved, smiling at Frank and Margy. He put down his brush and crossed over to them.

'Mornin', Frank. Mornin', Margy. You feelin' OK after the happenings?'

Frank tried to smile but was only partially successful.

'No, we ain't. I don't rightly know what to say, John. It's all still . . . well, I don't know what to say.'

Dawson nodded sympathetically.

'It's surely a terrible thing to have happened in your house, Frank. Say, would you like to come over to the store, both of you, and have a break?'

'That's kind of you, John,' said Margy. 'But we have to clear up. It's not every day someone's murdered in your house.'

'Murdered? More like exterminated.' Dawson's voice was angry and tense. 'You don't murder rats. You exterminate them. And Tucker was a murdering rat. Jack Farrow was a good friend of mine. I heard how that bastard murdered him in cold blood. He was . . .'

Frank noticed Deputy Sheriff James in the street and put his hand on Dawson's arm.

'Quiet, John. You don't want another rat to overhear what you're saying. Could be bad for your health. Terminally bad, you might say.'

# CHAPTER TWELVE

## PLOTTING

Sal was sitting on the rickety veranda of the old hut where she had a good vantage point to spot anyone approaching on the dusty track. Her Winchester was cradled on her lap and she tensed as she spotted the approaching horseman but when she recognized him she ran out to greet him.

Reuben dismounted wearily then unhooked a parcel from his saddle and dumped it on the veranda.

'A present from Margy. I guarantee it'll taste better than the beans I brought.'

After demolishing a large portion of the food hamper, they sat for a while enjoying a convivial silence, drinking a whiskey or two and enjoying the remnants of Margy's pie. When she had finished, Sal sat on the veranda, holding her knees and frowning. Reuben noticed her lips move on a couple of occasions, as if she was about to speak then thought better of it. When it happened for the third time he turned and faced her.

'Something's bothering you, Sal. Care to tell me afore

we call it a night?' He watched her troubled face and fell silent, waiting for her response. She took a deep breath and pursed her lips, as if she had just made a monumental decision.

'If you think it's hopeless, Reuben then you can ride out. I'll not think any the worse of you and no one else would either. You're not a fool and you know the odds.'

She looked at the ground to avoid eye contact and Reuben rolled and lit a cigarette and inhaled a lungful of smoke before replying.

'We're in this together, Sal. We need to sit and plan and rehearse then go over every tiny detail in our minds so we know precisely what we are doing when tomorrow arrives.'

Sal looked at the ground and then she nodded slowly.

'Thanks, Reuben. I was hoping you'd say that.' The relief in her voice was marked. 'So how do we go about planning? I'm a stranger to this sort of thing and I don't even know where to start.'

'Well, I wouldn't say that exactly. You seem to have started already. Anyway, as I see it we gather together all the information we know then we try to forecast what they will do. We've got to give ourselves as much of an advantage as we can. I've seen the town and there are quite a few places where they might hide. If they know we are coming then they have an even bigger advantage and to be honest, our chances then are slimmer than a hobo's wallet.'

'As I said, Reuben, if you—'

'We know we'll have to face six of them,' he interrupted. 'At least six of them. There'll be Cassidy and Robinson, Abe Coulson, Tom James and the two hired bodyguards, Eli Carson and Bill Pierce. It's Cassidy, Coulson and Robinson that we want to eliminate. They are the best killers. The others are just followers. You know what Cassidy and Robinson are capable of and you also know that Coulson's just about as good as a man can be with a gun. You'll know the three of them by sight so that gives you a split second advantage over them cos they mightn't recognize you at first, especially with what you'll be wearing. The others we need to nail simply because they'll kill us if we don't kill them first. Dog eat dog. Or in their case, rat eat dog.'

'That all seems logical. If we . . . hey, what d'you mean they won't recognize me cos of what I'll be wearing? Why ain't I going dressed like this?'

'We-ell,' Reuben drawled, with a faintly embarrassed smile, 'I reckon they'll be looking fer a woman dressed like yore dressed. When they see you you'll stick out like a sore thumb and be an easy target. Then I got to thinking what would happen if they didn't see you – or at least didn't recognize you. It might give you a couple of second's advantage. So I brung you these.'

He tossed a parcel on to the ground in front of her and she opened it slowly. It contained a gingham dress, a pert little bonnet and a parasol.

'I cain't wear . . .'

'Hold fire, Sal. Afore you start complaining just think about it. I walk up one side of the street and you on the other. You'll just look like a woman on her early morning walk to the store. They'll never look twice at you. By the time they realize you're there you'll be blazing away at them.'

The logic was irrefutable and Sal nodded, then she began to laugh and was joined in her merriment by Reuben. When eventually they fell silent she wiped her eyes and smiled at him. 'Where d'you get 'em? I guess someone might have noticed if you'd gone to the store.'

'They belong to Margy's sister. Margy said she left them there after her last visit and she's about the same size and build as you.'

Reuben still had grave misgivings. He knew that they were choosing the wrong time and the wrong battle ground but Sal was immovable. He knew that her motives weren't good ones in terms of tactics. She was being driven by the desire to avenge her husband. Reuben pleaded with her, giving her every argument he could think of to persuade her to postpone her mission but by the time he lay down on the floor near to where Sal lay on the creaky old bed he knew that her mind was set and he could do no more.

His mind juggled with the facts as he knew them. They had six pistols, including those taken from the Davies boys by Sal, and four Winchester rifles. They were all loaded. Cassidy may or may not know – and his bet was on the former – that they were coming for him. Even if he didn't know, the odds were still stacked overwhelmingly in Cassidy's favour.

He could hear Sal's rhythmic breathing and realized that she was asleep. His mind was whirling, weighing every alternative for the morrow but then his eyes felt tired and within minutes Reuben was asleep too.

An hour or so later, Sal opened her eyes and tried to remember where she was. She had been dreaming of Ed. In her dream they had both been working on the ranch and enjoying a fruitful day of labour before coming into the house for supper. When she woke she lay there for a moment, hoping that it was all true and that it was the horror of the past few days that was a dream. As she lay there, listening to the deep regular breathing of the sleeping Reuben, reality, unbidden and unwanted, came creeping back. Sal knew that she would probably walk to her death in just a few hours but she felt no fear, only a desire for what she hoped was justice but what she suspected was revenge. Knowing that the denouement was almost upon her she felt a strange, inexplicable wave of contentment for the first time since the awful moment when Shep Cassidy had arrived at her ranch.

*Her ranch!* For the first time since leaving it, she wondered what had become of the Crooked M. She was sure that Roy Gregory and the boys from the Lazy Gopher wouldn't let anything bad happen to her home, but for the first time, she began to feel homesick. She wanted to return to the place which she and Ed had tended and nurtured. Then her mind drifted back again to that awful day and she felt nothing but a desire to dispense justice, or indeed vengeance to Shep Cassidy and his murderous gang.

Sal had been thinking more about Abe Coulson in recent times. It was strange how he'd come back into her life. She'd still not been beaten to the draw by anyone else and somehow, in the back of her mind, she knew that she would have to face up to Coulson one last time. That would be the final act. The decider.

She crept silently from the room and stood outside looking at the vast, starry sky. It could – very likely *would* – be her last night alive. The first signs of light were beginning to show on the horizon. Reuben had agreed that they would go to Redwood at dawn, before Cassidy and his gang had surfaced.

The names of her protagonists drifted repeatedly and relentlessly through Sal's mind. Shep Cassidy. Abe Coulson. Tom James. Crazy Pete Robinson. Eli Carson. Bill Pierce. Any one of them would take great pleasure in killing her later in the day if they were given any chance. And she had to admit to herself, she would take satisfaction in killing them and finally achieving justice for her husband.

When dawn came they drank hot, strong coffee and ate some bacon before setting out for Redwood. It would be light when they arrived in the town, although the townsfolk wouldn't have surfaced. They had arranged that on their arrival in town they would dismount and walk along the covered walkways which would afford them some cover from anyone hiding in an upper storey window. Sal, in her dress and bonnet, would walk on one side of the street and Reuben on the other. Reuben said he was fairly confident that they wouldn't be expected. He didn't fully believe what he said. Neither did Sal.

The sky was beginning to pale as they rode on in silence and Reuben couldn't stifle the foreboding which he felt. He still wasn't sure how he'd respond in a gunfight with Sal at his side. He knew that his feelings for her were growing more intense, even though he also knew that he could never have her. Being at her side in a deadly gunfight when he felt what he felt for her was a dilemma which he hadn't foreseen. Would he forget all the rules and instead try to ensure her safety? Would she freeze again and be a liability rather than an asset? She was a complication. For a moment he even considered the possibility of forcibly removing her guns and taking her horse and riding on to Redwood alone but it was stupid idea.

116

So he rode in silence, juggling the possibilities in his mind.

'What are you thinking, Reuben? You've not said a word since we left the hut.'

He partly explained his fears, omitting to mention his worry that she might freeze. She listened in silence, staring straight ahead. When he finished speaking, she turned her head towards him.

'I'm coming along, Reuben. End of argument. Two guns are twice as good as one.' And the tone of her voice made it clear that the discussion had ended. 'Do you really think they'll not be waiting for us, Reuben?'

Reuben rubbed his stubbly chin and frowned.

'I ain't sure, Sal. My hunch is that they won't but Cassidy ain't stupid and between him and Abe they might have worked it out by now. If they have worked it out. . . .' His voice trailed away. The thought that Cassidy would be waiting to ambush them didn't bear thinking about, but they had to be prepared. 'If they *are* waiting for us they'll be facing this way. That's why it will be to our advantage if we circle round town and come at them from the back.'

The words didn't sound convincing, even to the speaker, but he could not stop Sal and he couldn't let her go to certain death alone.

The sun was peering over the horizon as they finished circling and rode into Redwood.

# CHAPTER THIRTEEN

## FRANK

At the same time as Reuben and Sal were bedding down for the night in the hut, Frank was staring up at the faces of Shep Cassidy and Crazy Pete Robinson as they leaned over his bruised and battered face.

'OK, Frank. If you ain't going to tell us, we'll start work on yer wife.'

Robinson spun on his heels and smashed his fist into the wall next to Margy's head.

'How do you think she'd look with no teeth, Frank? I'm sure I could do a bit of dentistry. In my own style of course.' He laughed at his own joke. 'How about it, Frank? Time for me to improve yer wife's teeth?'

The threat to his wife was too much. Frank broke down. He would tell them what they wanted to know.

'So, Frankie boy. Tell us. It'll be good to see Reuben Kane 'n' that whore agin. I got a couple of scores to settle with them.'

Within minutes, they knew about Reuben and Sal and they also knew that the pair were coming to town. The only part of the equation that Frank didn't tell them was the time. He said that he reckoned Reuben and Sal would arrive at noon. He hoped that it would be a vital detail.

Cassidy nodded at Robinson.

'We'll be ready fer 'em!' he growled.

'What about these two?' Robinson nodded at Frank and Margy and placed his right hand on his sidearm. His intention was clear and for a moment Shep Cassidy looked on in agreement. Then he shook his head.

'They cain't do us no harm. Leave them be. Let's go and round up the boys.' It was a uniquely merciful moment in the life of Shep Cassidy.

As they left his house, Frank crawled to his wife and she cradled his head.

'God help us, Margy. If Reuben Kane can't stop them . . .' His voice faded and he stared into the frightened eyes of his wife. He felt helpless, hopeless and totally defeated.

'Damn it all, Margy. What the hell has it all come to? Living here at the beck and call of Cassidy. Living in a town where we're all too old or too damn scared to do anything.' He staggered to his feet, helped by his wife and she led him to the chair in the front of the house, overlooking the street.

'Stay there, you old fool and I'll get you something strong to drink. Might ease the pain a mite.'

Frank shook his head, staring pensively at the darkened street.

'It'll take more than a strong drink to ease the pain. A hell of a lot more.'

A few lights still flickered in the warm night and Dawson, ever present, was sweeping the area outside his shop, humming quietly to himself. He stopped and leaned his broom against the shop front and lit his pipe, glancing over at Frank and waving a greeting.

'Fine night, Frank. You enjoying the night air?'

Frank made to wave back but a sharp, savage pain in the ribs caused him to lurch forward, clutching his chest. Dawson ran across the street and put an arm round the old man's shoulders.

'Are you OK, Frank? Hell, what's happened to your face? You've more bruises than an old barrel of rotten apples.'

'Shep Cassidy. That's what happened.' The voice of Margy came from behind him and she pressed a glass of special Irish whiskey into Frank's hand before kneeling down in front of her husband. 'I'll get the doc over to see you, Frank, and he can give . . .'

'Don't fuss, woman!' Frank exclaimed, waving a dismissive hand. 'Ain't the first time I've cracked a rib or two and there ain't anything the doc kin do that we cain't do ourselves. A couple of these will help,' he added, before downing the whiskey in one gulp. Nevertheless, he winced as he straightened up and Dawson and Margy looked on with concern.

'So what happened? You say it was Cassidy?' enquired the shopkeeper.

'It was Cassidy all right. I'll fix up another whiskey for you, Frank. Care to join him, John? It ain't every night we get the best Irish out.'

'Well, thank you, Margy. I don't mind if I do.'

'I'll leave Frank here to tell you what happened.' She

looked at her husband with wifely concern. 'Are you sure you don't need the sawbones, Frank?'

'I'm sure. Another whiskey'll help though. A big one.'

For the next few minutes, John Dawson listened as Frank related the happenings which had led up to his beating. He didn't mention Reuben or Sal, except to say that there had been an ancient feud between Reuben and Pete Robinson. Frank reckoned that to give any more information could compromise the safety of Sal and Reuben.

Occasionally Dawson whistled softly in disbelief as the story unfolded.

An hour or so later, slightly mellowed by the whiskey, they sat staring at the sheriff's office over the street.

'Damn it, Frank. I sure wish I wuz twenty years younger.'

'Me too, John. But we're an old town of has beens and nothing we say'll do anything to improve things. Cassidy's got the town and us just where he wants us.'

'Nothin' truer. There ain't nothin' truer.'

# CHAPTER FOURTEEN

# BATTLE STATIONS

'We'll leave our horses here. We don't want anyone to see us riding in. Have you got your guns?'

Sal grinned in the gloom. Stupid question.

'Now where do you think a lady would hide two Colts and a Winchester, Marshal Kane?'

Reuben grinned back at her. She looked for all the world like a prim lady going peaceably about her business, her bonnet low over her eyes and her dress swirling as she walked. She turned to face him and in her hands she held what looked like a bulky shopping bag. It contained her guns. Another Colt .45 was tied loosely into her petticoat – not accessible with great speed but strategically handy.

'I'll take the right side of the street. You take the left. Keep your eyes peeled, especially in the upper windows and the roof spaces. Worth keeping your third eye focused under the sidewalk. It's a place I've hid in afore now. If we ain't been challenged before, I'll swing up onto the balcony of the saloon and enter Cassidy's bedroom the unorthodox way – by the window. You stay down here and go in the saloon through the front door. We gotta bank on them not recognizing you, which'll give you time to start shooting. I should be on the landing by that stage and they'll be caught in the crossfire.'

'Easy as fallin' off'n a log!' Sal smiled again. Curiously, she didn't feel nervous.

She surprised herself by leaning forward and giving Reuben a light kiss on the lips. It surprised Reuben even more.

'I'll see you for lunch, Marshal. Take care of yourself.'

She stepped into the dingy street and when she reached the sidewalk, she looked back and nodded. Reuben returned her signal by checking that his Winchester was ready for action then they both moved slowly, cautiously making their way down the street.

Lee Hing's restaurant was being prepared for the early risers who would need a breakfast and a single light flickered from the kitchen area, where Lee Hing was slicing chunks of white fat to go into the massive blackened frying pan which he would use to fry the bacon. Lee had worked out many years ago that the smell of bacon cooking would draw in hungry cowboys and anyone else looking for a temporary cure for a hangover, like moths to a flame. He placed eggs on a rack, ready to drop them into the pan with the bacon, and then he started to cut huge slices of bread, ready for buttering or frying. Lee Hing was oblivious to what was happening just a few yards from where he worked. Had he known, the restaurant would have been in darkness and he would have been quietly tucked up in bed.

*

Neither Sal nor Reuben knew that before they even reached town, Shep Cassidy had convened a meeting with his mob following the visit to Frank and Margy. The presence in Redwood of Reuben Kane was the sole item on Cassidy's agenda. The group sat around a table in the back room of the saloon. Pete Robinson was leaning back on a wooden chair, picking at his nails with a sharp knife and chewing on a cheroot. Every few seconds his weasel face would appear from under the sombrero and his dark eyes would flash round the room. Cassidy was pouring himself a whiskey and next to him sat Deputy Tom James, checking his sidearm by looking down the barrel and spinning the chamber. Eli Carson and Bill Pierce sat facing the door on the opposite side of the table. They were unused to being invited to meetings but with the deaths of Jed and Shorty Gambles and the unexplained disappearance of Rab and Johnny Davies, numbers were thin and Cassidy was a believer in ensuring that enough guns were at his disposal to deal with any situation that might arise.

They were waiting for Abe Coulson and Cassidy always became irritable when he was kept waiting. It was rumoured that he had once killed someone who was five minutes late for a meeting but the fact that he needed Coulson, coupled with the latecomer's speed and accuracy with his guns, ensured that Cassidy would not be planning to challenge him.

The door swung open and Coulson, immaculately dressed in his customary grey frock coat and a white silk shirt topped with a black bow tie, strode slowly to the only empty chair, situated to the right of Shep Cassidy. Cassidy nodded in a perfunctory manner, downed his drink and glared round the table.

'Now you're all here,' he glared pointedly at Coulson, who smiled serenely, 'we can decide how to rub out Reuben Kane.'

'And the woman.' It was Tom James who spoke. 'She's part of it.'

Cassidy glared at him and continued.

'We know that Kane has trailed us and we know he killed Jed and Shorty – or at least he was there – *and* he tried to kill me. He's got a woman with him. Sal McIntyre's her name. She's a sort of man-woman – buckskins and a man's hat and she's known to shoot too. John Dawson's spoke with her and Tucker persuaded him to part with a little information. We've bin told that they'll come at noon but my hunch is they'll be here earlier. I've arranged for Dawson to be up early and he'll give a signal – he'll light a smoke – if he sees anything.'

'So what's the problem, boss?' asked Eli Carson, who didn't see the danger of one man and a woman.

'The danger is that Kane is fast. He kills good. The woman I ain't sure about. Mebbe she's just his whore. Mebbe not. Whatever she is, we'll kill her.'

'Mebbe we could have some fun with her first.' The deputy saw the fierce expression on Cassidy's face and he paused in mid sentence. 'Sorry, boss.'

'We *kill* her. We take no chances. None at all.'

'OK, boss.' Suitably chagrined, James lapsed into silence.

'As I said, I think theys'll come early. If'n they do, we'll be waiting. Me 'n' Pete'll be in the Crazy Lady. Pete'll be

THE CROOKED M KILLINGS

lying on the roof outside of the window with a Winchester.'

He glanced round to ensure that his audience had understood. Satisfied that they had, he continued.

'Eli, Bill – there's two coffins standing leaning agin the front wall of the undertaker's. Stand in those and wait. You'll be able to see the street through the cracks. Anything suspicious, shoot and ask questions later.' He surveyed his companions again. 'Tom. Stay in the sheriff's office. Blast him from the window.'

Coulson blew a cloud of blue smoke into the air and smiled at Cassidy.

'And me? Where do you want me, Shep?'

'You're our wild card, Abe. You just go where you want to go. When you see 'em, you know what to do.'

Abe Coulson laughed a quiet, throaty chuckle.

'I sure do, Shep. I sure do.'

# CHAPTER FIFTEEN

## BREWING

Reuben was surprised to see light emanating from Dawson's Emporium. He smiled to himself and muttered to himself under his breath.

'I reckon you never sleep, John Dawson. A twenty-four hour pursuit of money six days a week and fifty-two weeks a year. Well, good luck to you. But keep to hell outta my way. The last thing we need is an innocent person walking into the firing range.'

He waved across the street at Sal, indicating for her to stop and check the street out for anything which might make her suspect that something was wrong. He looked along the rooflines for any signs of movement, then into the blackness underneath the walkways and the many doorways, searching for fleeting shadows. He observed the barrels grouped further down the street outside the Crazy Lady Saloon. He wasn't sure if any of them had been moved to create a hiding place for a would-be assassin. He kept the information at the front of his mind. It was only when he was as satisfied as he could be that he waved his hand to indicate that Sal could continue.

Sal too had been examining the street, her vision heightened by the tension which she was at last beginning to feel. A sudden movement in front of her caused her to reach into her bag and close her hand round the handle of her Colt, her finger placed lightly on the trigger and pointing the hidden gun to her front.

The noise was the door of Dawson's shop and he appeared with a sack of flour which he placed leaning against the doorway before pinning a price tag to the wall behind it. Dawson appeared to gulp in the morning air, and then he looked first one way, then the other, up and down the street. Sal could have sworn that he'd seen Reuben but if he had he showed no sign or desire to show any recognition. This bothered Sal. She had never fully trusted Dawson and now she wondered if he had in fact seen Reuben and why he had not acknowledged him. To her left she could see that a light was shining in Frank and Margy's house. It wasn't surprising, she reflected ruefully, that they were unable to sleep.

Reuben, on the other side of the street, had reached the sheriff's office in which Tom James was crouching behind the window sill, a Winchester rifle held tightly and nervously in his sweaty hands. On the sidewalk at the far side of the street James could see a lady dressed in a gingham dress and bonnet walking slowly and quietly. Strange. Why would a lady be out at this time of the morning? He wrestled briefly with this question but his limited intellect couldn't find an answer so he shrugged and reached to the stove to pour a mug of coffee from the old coffee pot. As he reached over he touched his hand on the hot surface and he yelped and knocked the pot off the stove, sending it clattering to the floor and spurting scalding liquid in all directions, some of it on to his hand. He cursed loudly. All thoughts of Reuben Kane were forgotten as he gripped his scalded hand and leapt to the cell, where he plunged it into a bowl of cold water.

'Sheeeesh!' he exclaimed as the cool water momentarily took the pain away. He shook his hand and blew on it before plunging it again into the bowl. The voice behind him caused him to spin around in panic. The door closed silently behind the unmistakable figure of Marshal Reuben Kane, who stood facing him with a Winchester rifle pointing at the deputy's stomach.

'Howdy, Deputy.'

Tom James stood in silence. He looked longingly at his rifle, leaning against the window sill and out of his reach, then stared at Kane and saw only coldness in his eyes. He knew that he was doomed. If Kane didn't kill him, Cassidy surely would when he learned of his incompetence. He began to shake and gabble.

'Good to see you, Marshal. I jest burnt my hand on the stove. Careless fool thing to . . .'

The sentence hung, unfinished, in the air. Kane didn't move a muscle. Beads of sweat glistened on Tom James's forehead.

'Give me one reason not to kill you, you son of a bitch. Just one.'

James was reduced to incoherent babbling. His terror was palpable. Had he been capable of thought he would have realized that Kane did not want to raise the alarm by shooting him. The gunfire would have Cassidy coming out shooting.

'OK, James. I'm gonna give you a chance. I'm gonna put you in your own cell and then I'll call fer a judge and we'll have a trial. Then, likely as not, we'll hang you.'

James nodded furiously. At least there would be a delay. And if Kane was killed he could say he was rushed and maybe, just maybe, Cassidy would let him off with his life. Kane took a pair of handcuffs from a hook on the wall.

'Get in the cell and put your hands through the bars. Behind you.' Kane handcuffed the deputy to the bars then he stuffed a piece of cloth into his mouth and gagged him with his own necktie.

'Now, not a sound, you no good bastard. If'n I hear so much as a peep out of you I'll be back and you'll find out what it's like to have a bullet in the belly. Do you understand?'

The killer was blubbering with terror and Kane looked at him contemptuously before locking the cell and walking towards the door.

'Remember. Not a sound.' Reuben's last view of Tom James's was the back of his head still nodding violently. He shut the door quietly behind him and walked out into the street.

Sal, standing in the shadows outside Frank's house, was frantic with worry. Reuben had been gone for a full five minutes and she didn't know if he was alive or dead. Her relief when he appeared in the doorway and gave her a wave was immense. He signalled silently that he was OK then he indicated for her to continue walking down the street.

Reuben was close to Dawson Provisions Emporium now and he could see Dawson's silhouette thrown by the light of the oil lamp in the window. Silently, he peered in through the doorway. Dawson was placing trays of coffee, spices and candies on the wooden counter, singing hymns to himself.

'Rock of ages cleft for me. Let me hide myself . . .' The hymn ceased abruptly when he dropped a fresh egg, which splattered in an oily yellow mess on the floor. 'Sh-sugar!' He straightened up and went into the back room to get a mop to clean the floor. Reuben took his chance and slipped past the doorway. He didn't know that Dawson had turned and seen him pass. Dawson leaned on the mop and a faint, secret smile played on his lips. If Reuben had seen him he would have been worried. Very worried.

Unaware that he had been observed, Reuben crept noiselessly along the wooden walkway towards the Crazy Lady. He was sure that he would find Cassidy in the saloon and his mouth turned dry at the thought of what was to come. He stopped at the end of the covered walkway. The building with the sign proclaiming that it was the home of the Carpenter, Joiner and Undertaker was the only structure between Reuben and the saloon and he studied it carefully. A small pile of wood lay in the street – too small to act as a hiding place. Two coffins stood on end, leaning against the signed wall but there was nowhere that Reuben could see that would act as a place of concealment. The undertaker's was the only building on this part of the street that wasn't fronted by a raised, canopied walkway and he looked across the street to where Sal was standing. There didn't appear to be anyone hiding either in the bedroom or under the walkway on her side but Reuben signalled for Sal to cross the street as her covered walkway had finished and she would be exposed walking opposite the saloon. He waved her forward, signalling, rather superfluously, for her to be extra cautious. With glacier-like slowness she edged forward, past the coffins and towards the Crazy Lady saloon. Neither of them noticed the lids of the coffins edge sideways, to afford their residents a breath of air and a slit view of the street. The first thing that Reuben heard was a crash as the wooden lids were thrown aside and Eli Carson and Bill Pierce appeared, guns blazing.

Reuben threw himself to the floor, twisting sideways and dropping his rifle in favour of the two Colts at his side. Tiny clouds of sand shot into the air where he had been lying as a hail of bullets slammed into the earth.

Eli Carson aimed again and his mind registered a vague curiosity as the woman in a dress walked calmly towards him. He fired at Reuben and realized, too late, why the woman was pointing her white bag at him. The bag exploded in an orange flash and Eli was thrown backwards with the power of the bullet smashing his left shoulder. He screamed in agony and turned his gun on the woman. His hand squeezed the trigger as the second bullet struck his forehead. His gun barked but he never saw the woman fall from the wound he had inflicted. He was dead before he hit the floor.

Reuben fired twice at Bill Pierce. Pierce himself fired high into the air before crumpling to his knees. He looked down at the two red stains spreading on the check material of his shirt then he pitched headlong into the dust, trying vainly to pick up his gun. He died before his grasping fingers could reach it.

Reuben turned to Sal. She was lying deathly still and for a fatal moment he forgot about Cassidy and the others. He stood up and ran towards her and he was faintly aware of the crack of gunfire a split second before a bullet creased his shoulder. He knew that he had made a bad, maybe fatal mistake and his instinct took over. He ran a few steps then flung himself onto the ground before rolling under the wooden sidewalk.

He lay there, not daring to make a sound. His wound was just a graze and he was more concerned about Sal. He looked out into the street. Sal sat up, clutching a wounded arm and began to rise to her feet.

'Sal!' he yelled. 'Over here! Run!'

He was too late. A fusillade of shots sprayed around her and the silence which followed was broken by the sound of Crazy Pete Robinson's voice. 'Stay still, lady. One more step and you're a dead woman!'

Sal looked up to where the voice was coming from and she realized that she had no choice. Out of the shadows walked Abe Coulson, smiling and looking relaxed, as if he had just wandered out for a stroll. In his hands were twin Colts, both pointing at Sal McIntyre.

'Do what the man says, lady.' He turned to where Reuben was hiding. 'Now, Marshal Kane, I'm giving you three seconds to come outta there. After three I shoot the little lady in the hip. After another three, I shoot her in the right knee. Another three, and her left knee. You get the idea?'

Reuben had no choice. He knew that Coulson wouldn't hesitate to carry out his threat. He could probably gun Coulson down from this distance but then Robinson would gun Sal down from the roof. He moved out into the street.

Coulson smiled and nodded complacently.

'I knew you'd see sense. Now walk over here, very

133

slowly. Throw your guns over to me then the both of you stand up where I can see you.'

By the time Reuben had complied with the orders, Shep Cassidy and Pete Robinson had joined them. Coulson holstered his guns and smiled.

'Well, I guess I'll leave you to finish this little bit of unpleasant business off, boys. It ain't my argument no more. I'll see you over in Lee Hing's when you've . . . er . . . cleaned up.' He turned to Sal, who was standing facing him and he tipped his hat. 'Pity we couldn't have met under different circumstances, ma'am. I reckon we might have got on fine together.'

Still smiling, Abe Coulson strolled across to have his breakfast at Lee Hing's. He had already put the events of the morning out of his mind.

# CHAPTER SIXTEEN

## EXITS CLOSING

'Abe!' Shep Cassidy called to the gunman, who turned back mid stride.

'What d'you want, Shep? I'm hungry.'

'Kin you go 'n' check on Tom? He was waiting in the jail house.'

As Coulson headed to the sheriff's office, Cassidy walked towards Sal.

'Now, you bitch, afore you go to meet your Maker, mebbe you'd like to tell old Shep just what in hell makes you want to kill me so much.'

Sal raised her head defiantly and gradual recognition began to dawn in Shep Cassidy's eyes. He frowned and squinted at the woman, and then the frown cleared, as if a mental mist was lifting.

'Hell, yeah. I remember seeing you now. Cain't fer the life of me remember where or when though and I always remember a purty face. I'm damned if—'

He was interrupted by Abe Coulson walking towards them with a dishevelled-looking Tom James.

'Look what I found, Shep. All chained up in his own jail. Trussed up like a chicken.'

James, fastening his gun belt, shuffled towards them.

'Weren't my fault, boss. They ju—'

'Shaddup, Deputy. I don't want to hear no excuses.' Cassidy clenched his fists and made a mental note to deal with the bumbling fool later.

Tom James, oblivious to the evil stare from Cassidy, approached Reuben with murder in his eyes then, as he raised his fist to strike him, Cassidy pulled him back angrily. 'Calm down, Tom. There's time enough fer that.' He waved in the direction of Sal. 'I was having a conversation with the pretty lady when you interrupted. I don't much like being interrupted.' The implied threat was not lost on Tom James, who immediately stepped back.

'And,' added Coulson, 'you stopped me getting my breakfast. I'll bid you good morning, gentlemen and goodbye to you, Mr Kane and you, ma'am.' He touched the brim of his hat, as if he was acknowledging a vicar after Sunday morning service, then he grinned, sighed and patted his stomach. 'You know what? All this excitement adds to a man's appetite.'

Coulson walked away, leaving Cassidy, James and Robinson facing the helpless Reuben and Sal.

'Now, where were we? Where in hell did I see you afore, ma'am?'

Sal stared at him, still defiant. Cassidy expected to see fear in her eyes but instead he observed nothing but contempt.

'You murdered my husband, you scum.' Sal growled rather than spoke. Cassidy glowered and stepped towards her, but she continued speaking. 'Does the Crooked M ranch mean anything to you?'

For a few seconds, Cassidy was nonplussed, then he smiled and the smile became a raucous laugh.

'Why, yes! Now I remember. How could I ferget? You were so, er, accommodating!' He turned to Tom James. 'Deputy. Perhaps you'd be good enough to deal with Mr Kane. I kinda think he's outlived his useful life.'

'My pleasure, Mr Cassidy. I can see that you and the lady are old friends.' Tom James spun his Colt theatrically on his trigger finger.

'I'll leave you and Pete to clear up.' Cassidy spoke casually. 'Kill Kane. You can use one of the two coffins over the road. Shame to waste them. I'd like the lady to see what happens to people who upset me. I think that seeing Kane meet his end'll be a good lesson fer her. So make sure she gets a grandstand view. When you've done, bring the woman over to Lee Hing's. It'll be good to renew old acquaintances.'

He leered and brushed Sal's cheek with his hand before turning away and walking towards the restaurant.

Tom James faced Reuben Kane and aimed his gun at the lawman's stomach.

'This ain't gonna be nice, Kane. Well, when I say it ain't gonna be nice, what I mean is that it won't be nice fer you. I'll kinda enjoy it.' He bent forward until his face was a few inches from Reuben's. 'But you sure as hell won't. Have you ever seen a man die that's been shot in the stomach?'

'Deputy James?'

It was Sal. Her voice was weak and wavering.

137

'I think I'm going to fai . . .'

Sal swayed, and then fell backwards on to the road.

'Damn it, woman!' He turned to Kane again. 'First, let me deal with you, Kane, the . . .'

He looked momentarily at Sal, who was lying on her back. She was raising the hem of her dress. For a moment he believed that the stupid bitch was trying to make him take his mind and eyes off the job and he sneered.

'You don't catch me like that, ma'am. You've got to be a damn sight sharper than that to catch old Tom James.' He turned again to Reuben and didn't see the Colt .45 appear from under Sal's dress. By the time his mind had registered what his eyes were telling him Sal had pulled the trigger twice. The force of the shots lifted Tom James into the air and he smashed down onto his back in the dry dust. He lay twitching and moaning.

Sal tried to turn the gun in the direction of Robinson, who had been observing dispassionately from the sidelines but the material of her dress caught up with the barrel and this caused a fatal split second delay. She saw to her horror that Robinson's pistol was aimed at Reuben from point blank range.

'Drop the gun, you bitch. If you don't, Kane gets it in the stomach. Drop the gun!'

'Don't do it, Sal. He's gonna kill us anyway. Shoot the murdering bastard!'

Sal's finger curled round the trigger, but after half a second her face seemed to crumple.

'OK, Robinson.' She spoke quietly and her voice had the tone of someone accepting that defeat was inevitable. 'You win. I'll put my gun down if'n you promise to let Kane walk away unharmed.'

'Sal! Don't be a fool!' Reuben's voice was desperate. 'Kill him now and one of us'll survive. If you throw—'

'Shut up, lawman. Let the lady make her own mind up. I'm a man of my word, ma'am. If I make a promise that I'll let you go, well, that's what I'll do.' He smiled at Sal. 'Whatever you may have heard, Pete Robinson always keeps his word, ma'am. Now why don't you throw that gun away so we can all walk away from this with no hard feelings.'

Reuben couldn't comprehend that Sal would believe what Robinson was saying, but to his amazement she slowly withdrew the Colt and tossed it into the street. Reuben remained stock still. He was shocked, stunned in his disbelief and he stared at Sal. Then he realized that she didn't look afraid. Not only that, she wasn't even looking at Robinson. Her eyes were fixed on some point further down the street.

'Well, ma'am. That was a mighty fine decision.' Robinson lit a cigarette but his gun never wavered, remaining firmly sighted on Reuben's stomach. 'Fine decision fer me, that is.' He laughed. A dry, creaky sound.

'But you said . . .'

'Aw, I know, ma'am. I said I'd let you both go. I am, as I think I mentioned, a man of my word. And I gave my word to Mr Cassidy that I'd put the lawman in one of them coffins over there. You see my problem? I believe it's called a dee-lemma or some such. Anyways, I decided to keep my word to Mr Cassidy.'

Sal, still not looking at Robinson, touched the wound on her arm and rose to her feet.

'Go on then, Robinson. Get it over with.'

'That's my intention.' Crazy Pete Robinson nodded at

her, wondering why she was looking in a different direction.

'Sorry, lawman. Time fer you to go.' And he flicked back the hammer on his pistol with his thumb.

# CHAPTER SEVENTEEN

# THE END

Reuben Kane braced himself for the inevitable. He didn't fear death. He'd lived with the possibility of meeting a violent end for years. His single concern was for the safety of Sal McIntyre.

He closed his eyes and heard the shot. He waited for the pain. There was none.

He opened his eyes and blinked. He was still standing. A cursory glance showed no signs of wounds. For a moment he didn't comprehend what was happening. He stared at Crazy Pete Robinson, who was kneeling before him, eyes wide with shocked surprise and a trickle of blood coming from the corner of his mouth. Behind Robinson stood John Dawson and Frank. Frank was carrying a Navy Colt, the barrel of which was still smoking. Dawson held a shotgun which was aimed at Robinson's back.

It was then that Reuben realized why Sal had been

looking past Robinson and why she had dragged out the negotiations with the outlaw. She had been buying time to let the shopkeeper and the old man get within shooting distance of the would-be assassin. Reuben stared at Robinson. His lips were moving as if he was attempting to say something but he could only manage a whispery, incoherent growl before pitching face down into the dust.

Reuben stood in amazed silence, still unable to believe what had happened. Then he shook his head and grinned.

'Real pleased to see you, Frank. You too, John.' It was all he could think of to say.

Then he strode over to Sal and put his arm around her.

'You hurt bad, Sal?'

'No.' She shook her head and showed him the upper part of her left arm, which had suffered a flesh wound. 'Just a scratch. I did more damage when I fell. I hit the ground so hard that I was out for a minute or two.'

'You had me worried there. I thought you were a goner.'

'You thought *I* was a goner? Seemed to me that it was the other way round.' They grinned at each other and Reuben gave the woman a hug. For a brief moment in time they clung to each other and when they parted they were still making eye contact.

Frank, Reuben, Sal and Dawson stood in a line in the hot dusty street, facing towards the low sun. The outlaws lay behind them, both of them dead. Reuben, following his training as a lawman, knelt down and automatically removed their sidearms.

'Let me have his gun belt and pistols, Reuben. I feel naked without them.' Sal grinned and strapped

Robinson's gun belt over her dress. The effect was both incongruous and comical.

People were beginning to gather in the street and John Dawson called to them.

'Clear the streets. Shep Cassidy and Abraham Coulson are loose and Frank 'n' me are going to give Marshal Kane and Mrs McIntyre a hand in clearing them out of Redwood.'

The small groups dispersed and Sal, Reuben, John and Frank checked their weapons. Frank, having finished the task, smiled. He looked ten years younger. His eyes had a fire in them and he spoke authoritatively.

'Lee Hing's. That's where they are. There'll be nobody else there at this time of the morning.' He turned to them as a commander might when leading his troops into battle.

'Let's go get them.'

Reuben placed a restraining hand on his arm and Frank stopped, looking a mite disappointed.

'Hang on there, Frank. There's no point in taking any risk. If they see us coming they'll be ready and waiting. Is there another entrance to Lee Hing's?'

'Sure. Round the back through the kitchen.'

'In that case—' Reuben was interrupted by the sound of horses. Two riders had emerged from the livery stables and they were heading out of town as fast as their steeds would carry them. Cassidy and Coulson.

'Damn their hides! They're giving us the slip. After them!' shouted Frank but once again Reuben's restraining arm remained in place. Frank looked at him, not under-standing.

'This is a job for me, Frank. I'll ride faster on my own.'

143

'Not *quite* on your own. This has always bin *my* battle and you ain't going anywhere without me, Reuben Kane.' It was Sal who was speaking and as usual Reuben knew that any argument would be futile.

'OK. But we ride at my pace. If you can't keep up I'll leave you.'

'We're coming along too, Reuben. If we can't keep up we'll follow you.' This time it was Frank doing the talking and Reuben saw a similar determination in his expression.

Reuben sighed and looked at the two men, before shaking his head in resignation.

'I guess I can't stop you both. If y—' But he never finished what he was going to say because Sal was already striding to the stables.

Shep Cassidy and Abraham Coulson had reached Ennerman Valley, a ghost town which had been deserted for some ten or more years. They had ridden fast to Ennerman and now they sat in the deserted saloon, smoking. They and their horses were tired and Cassidy had deliberately headed for Ennerman because he had used it in the past to hide out from the law and he knew it like the back of his hand.

Coulson was irritable and impatient.

'Why the hell didn't we take 'em when we could, Cassidy? We could've nailed them when the two old timers had the guns and Kane was disarmed. It was a fool idea to hightail it.'

'Mebbe you're right,' conceded Cassidy. 'But it could've gone the other way. No saying how many townsfolk had guns. The fact is that we're here now and we've probably got an hour afore they get here, what with them trailing

144

and us knowing where we wuz going. We've got an hour to set up and wait for them, or to carry on running till we lose them.'

Coulson peered out of the glassless window, weighing up the pros and cons. He took a deep drag on his cigarette and blew a cloud of smoke up into the dusty air.

'I say we stay and finish it one way or the other. We can both take Kane. The woman should be easy.'

'Huh!' was all Cassidy would say.

'Whaddya mean, "Huh"? Are you saying we can't finish off a woman?'

'I'm saying that there's more to her than you think. I'm beginning to remember. When we killed her husband she looked mean with a gun. Accurate. Fast. All I'm saying is that we shouldn't underestimate her.'

'And all *I'm* saying is that the two of us should be able to finish them. Especially as we'll be in hiding. If we decide who takes Kane out then it should be pretty straightforward. I say we toss a coin.'

Cassidy, having no other credible plan, nodded his reluctant agreement and pulled a coin from the leather pouch which hung from his belt.

'Your call.'

'Heads.'

'You win, Coulson.' Coulson grinned and ground his cigarette out with the ball of his foot.

'I'll take the woman.'

'Suits me. I'll take Kane.'

They decided to wait in the old saloon, which offered the possibility of using the balcony to their advantage. They crouched in silence, smoke curling from Cassidy's chewed cigar. Through squinted eyes they looked down

145

the tumbleweed dotted street, waiting for any sign of movement. Coulson noticed that Cassidy was sweating and he was concerned in case the big man was losing his nerve.

'Wait till they get to the old barber's sign. That's just in range with a Winchester. You aim at her, me at Kane. I don't reckon we should miss from here. Job done. Then we ride back to Redwood and see the two bastards who killed Robinson and James. I think we have a good bit of unfinished business with them and we'll make them a good example of what happens to people who cross us. It'll teach the rest of the town a lesson.'

They waited.

Reuben and Sal weren't travelling as quickly as they'd hoped. Cassidy and Coulson obviously knew the territory and they weren't giving easy clues to follow. Frank and Dawson were having no difficulty in keeping up with them. Since Dawson had decided to risk everything by not sending the signal to Cassidy when Reuben and Sal hit town at dawn, he felt that he had discovered a new strength.

They came to a shallow rise and approached the apex with caution.

'I reckon I know where they are heading,' said Frank. 'Ennerman. An old cattle town that died out when the trail drivers started using the trail to the north. Ennerman just faded away and it's a ghost town now. There ain't nothin' else for miles around. We should be there in about thirty minutes.'

'It could be that they've decided to hole up in Ennerman.'

Reuben's mind was ticking over, weighing up the possibilities.

'They may be waiting there fer a showdown. Mebbe they'll want to settle it once and for all. Coulson ain't a coward and Cassidy's got a lot to lose if he don't go back to Redwood. My guess is that they're regretting having left Redwood and they'll be waiting for us either on the trail or in Ennerman. Has anyone been there?'

'Sure have.' It was Dawson who answered. 'I took a wagon load of provisions there for Cassidy about a year ago. Never knew why.'

Atop the ridge, Reuben looked down at the trail which lay below them. He felt sure now that Cassidy would be waiting for them at Ennerman but nevertheless he still knew that they would have to be watchful and on their guard during the ride for any possible places for an ambush.

Sal was silent, riding alongside Reuben. She was quietly determined that Shep Cassidy would not see another day, even if it meant sacrificing her own life.

Reuben still knew that Sal McIntyre's burning desire for revenge spelt potential disaster for them but he didn't know how to raise the subject again. They rode slowly towards Ennerman, looking for any places which might provide the potential hiding places for bushwhackers. The approach to the town was flat and featureless, which was on the one hand to their advantage, inasmuch as there were few places for Cassidy and Coulson to surprise them. On the negative side, the lack of undulation, rocks and plant growth meant that if Cassidy and Coulson were at Ennerman, they would see them coming from a distance and would be well prepared to greet them on their arrival.

With every step, Reuben expected to hear the crack of a rifle. The town was just a few yards away from them. They were passing a deserted shack at the start of the street and Reuben was eying it suspiciously when a shot rang out and John Dawson pitched from his horse and lay groaning in pain.

In the saloon, a furious Coulson shouted at Cassidy.

'Too soon, you fool! We said we'd wait till they got to the barber's!'

He realized he had no option but to fight now, but part of their advantage was lost and Kane was still alive.

Another shot from Cassidy's rifle felled Dawson's horse and Frank dismounted and dragged the wounded man behind the shack to shield him from any more fire. Reuben and Sal leapt from their horses and as they hit the ground they rolled behind the shack just as another shot caused splinters to shower from the corner of the shed, inches from Sal's head.

'How's Dawson?' barked Reuben.

'Leg wound. Seems like flesh. I'll bandage him up then—'

'Stay with him. Me 'n' Sal'll go into town. The shot came from the building on the right with the big balcony. We'll go in the back. C'mon, Sal. There's only a couple of feet, they can see us if we run from the other side of the shack. You go first. Fast as you can and I'll follow.'

'You sure are good at giving obvious orders, Reuben.' Sal grinned through gritted teeth. '*Fast as you can.* Are you expecting me to take the slow route fer the good scenery?'

'Get gone.' He grinned back. 'And good luck. I'll be right behind you. Frank, when we start to run, open fire with your Winchester and keep firing till it's empty. It'll give us cover to reach the next building to them and get behind the water trough. When we get there, reload and then start firing again.' Frank nodded, grimly. Sal, then Reuben, ran from the shack and he opened fire, peppering the window where he thought Cassidy and Coulson were holed out. Reuben and Sal, covered by Frank's fire, reached the building next door and Reuben waved back from the safety of the end wall.

'Sal. If we go through the window and round the back, we can get to the side wall of the building where they're hiding.'

'And what then?'

Reuben was already climbing through the window and, hampered somewhat by her dress, Sal followed him. They found themselves in a gloomy, wooden building. Old tables and chairs, deep in sandy dust, stood forlorn and a piano, minus a front panel and some keys, were placed in a corner. It boasted two candlestick holders with back reflectors and some sheet music lay on the ground. Reuben walked quietly across the floor and opened the door at the back of the room. He found himself in a stable. There were drinking troughs to the right of him, dry and dusty now and dried out straw was piled high in one corner. As he stood surveying the room he heard a distant voice from the saloon. It was Shep Cassidy.

'We ain't coming out, lawman. You'll have to come in and get us. We ain't goin' nowhere. We're waiting for you. Come and find us.' The last sentence was in a sort of singing voice, like a child mocking someone in a game. Sal moved up to Reuben's shoulder.

'Well? What are we waiting for? Let's go get the bastards. It's now or never, Reuben.' But Reuben shook his head and held her arm.

'That's precisely what they want us to do, Sal. They'll be

149

holed up in there with their guns trained on the door. They'll be hidden – behind the bar maybe or some furniture – and they'll blast us away as soon as we go in the door. By the time we've spotted them we'll have more holes than a pepper pot. No, we need to get them out into the street so we stand a chance. If we go in now we'll be giving them everything they want.'

'So how are we going to get them out into the open? Offer them candy?' asked Sal, impatiently. She suspected that Reuben was right but a mixture of anger, fear, frustration and tension was interfering with her thought processes.

Reuben looked thoughtful. His clinical mind was whirring and a plan was beginning to formulate. He moved towards the window and looked out into the street. Nothing moved except for the odd ball of tumbleweed and one tiny skittering lizard. He felt Sal's body leaning against his back, then he heard Abe Coulson's voice.

'Are you scared, Kane? Are you scared of what we'll do to that pretty lady after we kill you? Are you brave enough to come and get us, Marshal? Or are you all wind and noise? Are you scared to answer?'

Reuben felt Sal's body move as she prepared to shout a reply and he turned and clamped his hand over her mouth.

'Quiet!' he hissed. 'They don't know where we are and they are trying to make us answer so they can find out. We just keep quiet and say nothing. Let them get nervous. Understand?' Sal nodded from behind his hand and he let her go.

'What now, Reuben?'

'We get them out into the street. These buildings are as

dry as tinder. There's candles on the piano and the stable is full of straw and old sacks. Candles plus straw plus a flame from my matches equals fire and a lot of smoke. Let's go.'

They spent the next few minutes loosely filling sacks with dry, crackly straw then Reuben signalled to Frank to open fire again and under the cover of his fire they heaved three sacks of burning straw through the back door of the saloon.

Reuben was right. The building was a tinder box. Flames licked up the old curtains and the breeze from the open door fanned the flames into an almost instant inferno. Within minutes the flames had reached the front part of the building – once the bar – where Cassidy and Coulson were hiding.

'What the?'

Cassidy and Coulson both realized that there was no chance of beating back the flames.

'Get the hell outa here!'

The two men, eyes streaming, staggered into the street and they were faced with Reuben Kane and Sal McIntyre. Cassidy raised his gun but Kane was already poised and the fat man saw a gold rod of flame spurt from the barrel of Reuben's Colt, then he felt a searing pain in his chest. As he spun around the gun barked again and Shep Cassidy was catapulted over a rotting wooden box which had been left in the street. He fell face down in the dust and briefly, very briefly, he moved his head in one last effort to raise himself. Then he lay still. Shep Cassidy was dead.

Abe Coulson flung himself to the ground behind Cassidy, deliberately ensuring that he was half covered by the man's gigantic frame. He aimed at Kane and fired. Reuben, seeing Abe's intention, leapt sideways to try to gain the cover of a rotting hulk which had once been a wagon. Coulson's bullet thumped harmlessly into the wood and Reuben swung himself upwards and pulled on the side of the wagon to haul himself up into an advantageous position. There was a dull cracking sound and the rotten wood crumbled in his hands and he toppled backwards, smashing his head on a solid wooden crate. He lay there. Unconscious. It was a cruel twist of fate.

Sal stared at him, horrified. She thought he had been hit and shouted his name.

'Reuben! Reuben! You OK?'

She started to move towards the inert figure but her progress was halted by a fusillade of shots as Coulson used his pistols and those which he had taken from Cassidy. Sal lay flat and out of sight and there was, for a moment, silence.

'You there, ma'am? You there?' Coulson was calling as he reloaded three pistols.

'I'm here, Coulson. I'm here and I'm ready to kill you. You won't get the better of me this time.'

Coulson finished loading and looked for any sign of movement. Nothing. He guessed he must have hit Kane, but he knew that the lawman was a cunning old fox.

'What do you mean, "this time"? Have we met before? I'm sure I'd remember such a pretty face.'

'We met. We met a long time ago. You were a skunk then and you're a skunk now, Coulson.'

'We met before? Where? When?'

'If you cain't remember then I ain't going to refresh your memory, you vermin. Why don't you show yourself,

152

like the big tough *hombre* you pretend you are? Or do you think you ain't tough enough to take one woman in a fair fight?'

There was silence, then Sal continued her goading.

'Well, Coulson. Are you too afraid to face a woman on equal terms? Is that what the great Abe Coulson is about? A yellow, snivelling coward who can only shoot old, unarmed men?'

'What the hell're you talking about, madam?'

Sally laughed loud and long. She knew by the tone of his voice that she was beginning to needle Coulson.

'The great Abe Coulson. Nothing but a yellow belly. Scared to come out and face one woman. And just to think that people thought you were a man with guts.' She laughed again, hoping that her laughter sounded scornful and not scared.

The silence that followed was long and fearful. It lasted for a full minute and the minute seemed like an hour. Finally, Coulson shouted out.

'If you want a showdown, then show yourself. I'm prepared to give you an equal chance. Straightforward draw. Fastest wins and walks away.'

Coulson knew he would win. It was almost as if his prayers had been answered. Fighting like this, it was a matter of luck as much as judgement as to who got the all important shot in. Standing in the street face to face was a different matter. His territory. He smiled to himself.

'I'm gonna show myself. And I want you to do the same. Then we'll walk to the centre of the street and then I'll kill you in a fair fight.'

Slowly, tentatively, they both rose from their positions. Coulson first, then Sal edged to the centre of the street and there they stood, facing each other, he in his trade-mark frock coat and Sal in a dress with a gun belt strapped around her waist.

'I guess this is it, Coulson.' Sal's tone was emotionless. 'I guess I always knew it would be. As soon as your name was mentioned I knew we'd have to sort our unfinished business.'

'Unf—' Coulson started to speak but Sal interrupted him.

'Unfinished business. You remember going to a Wild West Show and drawing against a woman sharpshooter? Just afore you killed an old man in cold blood? Does that help you recollect what I'm talking about?'

The dawning light crept into Coulson's eyes.

'Sally . . . Sally. . . .' He searched his mind for the elusive name. She provided it.

'Seddon. Sharpshooter and quickest draw in the West. That's me, Coulson. Or it was me. I was just a girl then. I guess I might be faster now.' She paused for effect. 'D'you think I'm faster? Faster than you?'

Coulson smiled. He looked relaxed and confident as he stood there, hands hanging loose by his side. He shook his head slowly.

'I don't think so, Sally. In fact, I think you just made the biggest mistake in your life. And it's the last one you'll ever make.'

The silence in the street was broken only by the faint rustle of a breeze stirring the sand as the protagonists faced each other for one last time.

Behind Sal, Reuben started to regain consciousness and he groaned. Coulson, thinking that he might have walked into a trap, drew his pistol but his eyes were in the direction of Reuben Kane. Like lightning he redirected towards Sal but his hesitation was enough. Before he could squeeze the trigger two shots from Sal McIntyre's pistol found their mark. They were shots as good as any she had fired in her sharpshooter days. Mortally wounded, Abe Coulson staggered backwards, his gun blazing harmlessly into the sky. He looked blankly, disbelievingly at Sal, then he tried to aim his gun for one last shot. All he achieved was to send a bullet into the stony ground, then he fell backwards and lay there, almost motionless but gasping like a landed fish.

Cautiously, Reuben and Sal walked towards the bodies.

The tension and hatred left Sal like the morning mist being driven out by the sun. Up till now she had seen monsters with guns. Now she saw a man dying in the street. She felt no sadness or remorse and for the first time since Ed's death, she felt no hate.

Coulson was trying to say something but she would never know what. He looked up at her and she thought for a moment that there was a flicker of a smile, then his head fell back and he lay still. Maybe he was glad it was over.

# CHAPTER EIGHTEEN

# THE CONCLUSION

Sal McIntyre sat on the veranda of the Crooked M ranch watching Reuben Kane saddle up his horse. Three months had passed since the shooting. Three months of relief, guilt and nightmares, mixed with a gradual return to the normal routines, frustrations and pleasures associated with the day to day running of the ranch. Reuben had been worth his weight in gold and he had a natural aptitude for assessing priorities, planning and sheer hard graft. They had formed the perfect team and at the end of the day, as the sun sank on the horizon, they had spent many hours talking and exorcising the ghosts of Shep Cassidy and Abe Coulson. They were relaxed with each other. Natural and having nothing to prove after all the experiences they had shared.

Not once had they spoken of the feelings which they had for each other, except for occasional comments about how they valued their friendship.

156

Back in Redwood a new sheriff had been appointed and John Dawson was the new mayor. Reuben had resigned his post as marshal and then he had insisted on riding back with Sal to be with her until she settled back in on her ranch. Now the time had come to go.

Reuben didn't turn as he adjusted the straps on his saddle. He knew that he was going to miss Sal but he also knew that he couldn't stay and expect her to share the Crooked M, which had been the source of so much pain and hard labour for both Sal and the man who was buried a short distance from where he stood. He was aware of Sal's intense stare, her eyes boring into the back of his skull.

Sal, for her part, didn't want to force any issues. She felt intensely close to Reuben but she reckoned that it would be strange if she didn't feel close to him, given that they'd relied on each other to survive. For all of that, she still missed Ed and wondered how she would have felt towards Reuben if Ed had not been murdered. In those circumstances, she told herself, she would not have even noticed Reuben Kane.

Then again, she reasoned, this was not those circumstances. Those circumstances had ceased to exist the day that Shep Cassidy rode into the Crooked M.

Reuben took one last look at the ranch and grinned a sort of shy grin in Sal's direction. For reasons which neither of them understood, they had made no attempt to embrace and now he turned his back for the last time and slowly began to ride out of Sal's life forever.

'What'll you do?' she called after him, realizing that they had never discussed his plans for the future.

He tugged on the reins and the horse stopped. Her

question hung in the air and he too realized that although they had agreed that he would leave once the ranch was up and running, they had never discussed where he would go.

She had spoken without moving. She looked up at him from the chair on the veranda and her voice still gave nothing away. Her facial expression was equally enigmatic.

'I'll head back East.' He tried to sound matter of fact. 'I got relatives who I ain't seen for years. I'll stop with them awhile. Now I know you can get on without Ed. . . .'

He tailed off and there was silence and still without turning his head, he kicked softly on the flanks of the horse, waved over his shoulder at her then began to ride away. The sun was low in front of him and he adjusted the brim of his Stetson. He reached the gate and leaned down from his saddle to remove the thick rope which was looped over the gatepost. The gate creaked open.

'Damn gate. I meant to fix that hinge.'

He slung the rope back over the post and looked back towards the ranch house. Sal was standing on the veranda, hand shielding her eyes from the sun. She stepped down and started walking purposefully towards him and he sat astride his mount, waiting patiently and admiring the grace of her stride.

'Reuben!' Her voice had a different tone to it. Urgent. Almost fearful. She reached the fence and leaned her arms on it, looking up at him. He was silhouetted in the sunlight and she couldn't see his face. For his part he could see that she looked troubled and agitated.

For a second she stood in silence, her mouth slightly open. She wasn't sure what to say. Emotions were tumbling over themselves and she gasped for air slightly. She stared hard at the silhouette. Then she took a deep, decisive breath.

'I'll miss you, Reuben Kane.'

'And I'll miss you, Sal McIntyre.' He wondered if she knew how much.

He grinned again, turned his horse and started to ride away again.

'Reuben!' Her call was more urgent this time.

'What now?' He turned back to face her in mock annoyance.

'Stay.'

She stared at his silhouette, unable to gauge his reaction.

They were silent. Neither of them knew if they could stay together after all they had been through. Maybe they had been broken as people with the violence and death. Maybe Reuben Kane would always be a lawman and the idea of settling on a ranch would pall and ultimately collapse. Maybe Sal would forever hanker after Ed, longing for the husband who had been torn so cruelly from her. Maybe being together would constantly remind them of the awfulness of the past few weeks.

Maybe.

Life was full of maybes.

Reuben sat facing Sal and she repeated her words.

'Stay. Please. I'd like you to.'

He climbed down from his horse. When he enfolded Sal in his arms their embrace was natural, full of tenderness and relief. For perhaps the first time in his life, Reuben Kane felt at one with the world. At home. This, he told himself, was how life should be.

Sal looked up into his eyes.

'I'd like you to stay more than anything else. I don't know if it'll work, but I do know that I can't imagine a life without Reuben Kane at my side.'

Reuben smiled tenderly.

'And I don't want to even think of life without you, Sal. Of course I'll stay.'

They spent the evening in blissful contentment sitting on the veranda watching the sun sink in a big golden ball over the horizon. As the last signs of the golden orb sunk out of sight, leaving a stunning, golden orange sky, Sal leaned on the veranda rail. Reuben was in the kitchen.

Following Ed's murder, Sal had not believed that she would ever feel happiness again and now she stared at the sky and took a deep breath of the night air. She looked up at the same sky that Reuben had seen when he had nursed her back to health and she felt a deep, deep contentment.

'You coming in, Sal?'

'I'll be there directly.'

She stared at the small wooden cross, almost invisible in the gloom, which marked the spot where Ed lay.

'Goodnight, Ed.' And she turned and walked into the kitchen.